BUILT TO LAST
A LIFETIME

A NOVEL OF OLD KENTUCKY

BOOK ONE
LOST IN THE WILDERNESS

BOOK TWO
REEDS IN THE WILDERNESS

ELIZABETH DURBIN
AND
ERNEST MATUSCHKA

E Lizabeth Durbin

BUILT TO LAST A LIFETIME

Published for Durmat Associates by
OPA Publishing
Box 12354
Chandler, AZ 85248-0023

Printed in the United States of America

opa

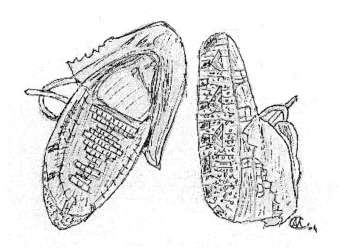

TABLE OF CONTENTS

BOOK ONE

TABLE OF CONTENTS

BOOK TWO

INTRODUCTION

To the Reader:

This is a novel of old Kentucky, set in the late 1700s or early 1800s, at about the same time that Daniel Boone was making his reputation. It was a time when people from the eastern states could move into the Kentucky territory and stake a claim on land, provided that they built a shelter, cleared some land, and raised a crop.

This is a historical novel, which means that the history and setting are accurate but the people are fictional. The dialect used in this book reflects the language style that was spoken by the early settlers in Kentucky.

It should be noted that while there is adventure in this book, there is a minimum of descriptive violence and an absence of sexual content. It is written for students from grades four through high school or for anyone who may enjoy a book of high interest and lower vocabulary levels.

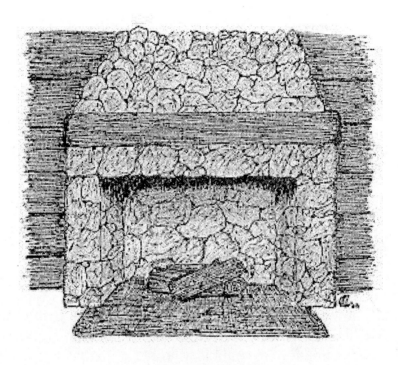

CHAPTER ONE

A FEELING IN HER BONES

Sarah knew she should get up. It was still dark outside, but Gramma was up and stirring the fire. There was a full day's work for her. At age fourteen, Sarah was expected to work like a grown woman. As she lay in bed, she thought of her mother, Lizabeth. Her mother was her role model and someone that she admired. It pained Sarah to remember her mother, since she had died of a fever last fall. Sarah never felt so alone or vulnerable. She loved her mother, and no words could describe the loss she felt.

The burden of raising the family fell on Sarah and Gramma. Gramma was her mother's mother. She was of good German stock, having arrived in Pennsylvania from Germany. Grandpa Asa was also German and would correct anyone who called him Pennsylvania Dutch. He would say, "We ain't Dutch, we are German."

Hard work was expected of Sarah. She had taken over the raising of the two younger children, Ben and Mary. Ben was a three-year-old who was into exploring everything. He could be made to mind, but most of the time he was off looking for excitement. Mary was two, and his shadow, as they were constant companions.

"Sarah, Sarah."

"Yes, Pa."

"Sarah, it's time to get up," Pa whispered.

"Yes, Pa. I'll get right up." Sarah stepped out of bed onto the cold floor. She stretched and yawned. She was becoming a tall girl, like her mother. Lizabeth was tall and muscular. Sarah had Lizabeth's blond hair, except Sarah's hair was a deep gold. Both parents, as well as all the children, had deep blue eyes. Sarah slipped off her nightgown and, turning her back to the room, slipped on her dress. Her first job in the morning was to make the corn meal mush ready for breakfast. If there wasn't enough corn meal, Sarah would have to grind some.

"Is Nathan up?" asked Pa.

"I don't reckon," Sarah replied.

The household was still dark and getting ready for dawn. They didn't light candles in the morning. A waste, Gramma would say, as candles were in short supply. In fact, almost everything one used over the winter was becoming in short supply.

Gramma always busied herself getting the fire going. She rarely talked in the morning, which Sarah missed, as she and her mother had usually kept a running conversation going from dawn until dusk. When Sarah thought of her mother and a baby sister she really never got to know, she developed a sharp pain in her stomach.

Pa would get up and head out the door to take care of the outside chores. Sarah knew that he would visit the graves every morning, and she knew that he was still grieving. This was a sad family, trying to survive the winter and make it into spring. Only Nathan seemed to be in good spirits most of the time. He was all boy and loved to hunt and fish. He was too young to go off into the forest alone and hunt, but he could go down to the creek and fish when the ice melted. At almost thirteen, Nathan was developing into a fine young man.

Sarah appreciated Gramma's silence. She knew that as soon as Gramma started talking she would begin demanding work out of everyone. It wasn't long.

As she laid aside her mending, Gramma said, "Land sakes, Luke, seems like a body just can't keep up with all the work that's to be done just to keep body and soul together around here. Looks like it should be warm enough that the dandelions will be up under the leaves to make a mess o' greens. My old mouth is lookin' for the taste of fresh greens."

"I've been thinkin' on it, Gramma. If I take it easy, I can go over the ridge and see if I can scare up a deer. The young'uns are needin' meat. I should've gone earlier, but now the snow is gone, I can go without fearin' that my foot will be froze again. If it's a good sky tomorrow, I'll go early, probably right before sunup. I might have to go a long way to find one, so don't worry if I don't get back 'fore three or four days. If I get a good buck, it'll take me that long to pack it back." Luke leaned over a shot pouch he was mending and looked at Gramma.

"You be careful, Luke," she said. "I heard a screech-owl last night and the night before. That ain't a good sign. I don't know how the little ones and I could do without you. Do you want me to fix some food to take with you? Land knows, there ain't much, but I could find you a few pieces of jerky I saved back in case we had more bad weather."

"A couple of pieces of jerky would be fine. Tomorrow Nathan can go down to the stream and cut him a pole. I'll fix him a fishhook, and he can try to catch some fish for you. Now that the ice is broke, maybe he can get some. They would taste mighty good."

Luke limped over to the shelf on the wall and got down the mold to make lead balls for his rifle.

Gramma watched him anxiously. His foot still wasn't right from when he froze it in the blizzard, she thought. She wished Luke wouldn't go, but they needed meat. She couldn't explain the feelings that she had. Luke would think she was just a foolish old woman if she would tell him. Something was not right. But try as she might, she couldn't put down the feelings of dread.

❧

Gramma was usually strong-hearted. She'd walked over the mountains with Luke and Lizabeth. She had kept her pace, carried her heavy load, and never regretted leaving the home place in Pennsylvania to come to this wilderness. But since the sickness that took Lizabeth and little Beth, she just couldn't take heart. Seemed like something in her went with them.

Well, she'd better put the starch back in her backbone, she thought. She'd have to take care of the young'uns until Luke got back. They'd all feel better when they'd got a bellyful of meat.

"I'm just worn out, tired, hungry and old. When you get old, you get fancies," she told herself as she rubbed her old, gnarled hands together.

Stiffly, she got up from the stool by the fire and went over to make sure that Ben and Mary were covered against the cold that would come when the fire died down. Her hand lingered over the quilt she had made from many different pieces of fabric left over from clothing that earlier she had made for her family. She cherished the quilt for its memories. She smoothed it with a calloused hand and remembered . . . that piece had come from the dress she wore when she married Asa; this one from a dress she had made for Lizabeth when she was three.

Lizabeth had said the quilt was too heavy to pack on her back over the mountains, and Gramma had almost agreed, but now she was glad she had carried it. It was a reminder of her husband, Asa. She remembered his tall, lean, muscular body even as he grew older. They were both hard working and were aware of each other's stubbornness. But Asa, with his long gray beard and twinkling blue eyes, had loved her deeply, and she felt his loss.

She had better go to bed. Tomorrow she would use the last of the fat to make soap. She had put it off too long, and they were running short. "They might be hungry, but they'd starve clean," she muttered to herself. She went outside for one last look at the stars. "It says in the Bible that the Lord watches over us. I've got Asa watchin', too. It won't be long 'til I'll be with him. I'll just have to wait a little while longer, 'til Nathan and Sarah and Ben and Mary are a little older." The two older children can almost take care of themselves, but Ben's a bundle of energy and Mary will need some extra care. It's unfair to Sarah to saddle a fourteen-year-old with being a mother to two babes, but the times dictate her life.

She checked once more to assure herself that two blond heads were poking out from under her quilt. "Good night, dear grandchildren," she whispered.

Gramma went to the bed she shared with Sarah. Nathan was asleep in the loft. Soon, Luke would join him. Peace was settling into the cabin.

The fire flickered as Luke took the melted lead and carefully poured it into the mold. Gramma didn't like the way the flames flared up. Another sign? "Old foolishness!" she sniffed, and rolled over, courting sleep.

CHAPTER TWO

DAYBREAK

Shortly before daylight, she heard the owl again. A shiver ran down her spine. She pulled the covers closer about her. In spite of her fear, she muttered, "Old foolishness."

The fire was blazing brightly. Luke must be up and gone. It was sun-up already. Quickly, she got out of bed. Her bare toes curled back from the cold, plank floor. Again, a shiver ran down her back. "Silly old woman!" she said out loud. There was no sign of Luke, and it looked to be a good day.

"There's no use wastin' time," she thought. She started cooking a pot of thin mush and brushed the hearth. Ben and Mary, both awake, sat with matted hair and shining, bright blue eyes, waiting for their breakfast. They were well-mannered youngsters and knew to be patient with Gramma, who moved as fast as she could.

Since Lizabeth's death with the baby, Ben, a natural clown, and Mary provided Luke with a lot of love. Both were loving children, and they provided entertainment for the family. Neither Ben nor Mary remembered their mother. So Gramma and Sarah were substitute mothers—not that either of them minded.

There were potatoes in the coals, and she raked one out carefully. One could not be too careful with hot coals in a wooden building. If the floor caught fire . . . well, Gramma didn't want to think of that. Instead, she fantasized about the fish that Nathan would catch and how good they would taste instead of just potatoes and mush. If they were careful, the corn would hold out until the new crop came in. They would have to piece it out with whatever they could find in the woods. She shivered again. "Somebody's a-walkin' over my grave," she muttered.

"Well, they'll just have to walk." She shrugged off the bad feeling as she got the old bucket off the shelf. She started down to the stream for water, thinking, "It's time to get the soap goin'."

Uneasily, she looked about her as she walked down the hill. She heard the owl again. It was now broad daylight, and owls don't hoot in broad daylight. "Maybe he got his time mixed up," she thought.

When she came back from the stream, the children were sitting on the stoop with their bowls of mush. They were the picture of innocence.

"It's a pretty day, Gramma," said Sarah. "I guess the dandelions are sleepin' under the leaves, just waitin' to be picked. Soon's I finish this and clean up the dishes, I'll go and see if I can find a mess. I can taste 'em already."

"Our bodies need greens," Gramma replied.

"Pa said for me to try to get some fish," said Nathan. "I'll get you some wood chopped up, Gramma, and then go down to the creek. You get the big, black iron skillet out, 'cause were goin' to feast today. I can feel it in my bones," Nathan teased.

Gramma was well pleased with Sarah and Nathan. At fourteen and almost a woman, Sarah was Gramma's best help.

She looked like her mother, Lizabeth. Deep blue eyes and flaxen hair, tall and thin. Gramma saw a real beauty in Sarah.

Nathan was almost thirteen, but he was taking on the work of a man. He was short and stocky, much like Gramma was. He would grow into manhood being of average height and broad shoulders. Gramma knew he came from good stock and would become a fine, responsible man. He was already doing tasks that were meant for adults. But as times were, he had to.

"I feel something in my bones, too," said Gramma. "You all stay close to the cabin. Don't know what it is, but somethin's not right. Your Pa has gone for meat. You get your faces washed and get your work done. Nathan, you go to the creek, but keep a sharp eye out. Sarah, you go up behind the cabin for greens, but stay close. Don't know what it is, but somethin' in my bones says there's somethin' in the air that ain't right." She went into the cabin to dress the young'uns and finish her chores before she started making soap. She needed to get Ben and Mary playing with their homemade toys in the corner of the cabin.

Gramma put the wood ashes into the hopper, poured water over them, and went to the creek to fill her bucket again. Nathan was half asleep against a big rock. She smiled at the sight of his gaunt body at ease, for once. "Guess he missed his mama more than he let on," she mused. Soon, all too soon, he would have to take a man's burdens on his shoulders.

She thought of Luke as she rolled her long, gray hair into a tight bun. Luke seemed crushed by Lizabeth's death. They had known each other since they were children in Pennsylvania, attending the same school and same Lutheran church. Gramma knew that Luke was grievin' every day, as was she. He had lost a wife; she had lost a daughter; they both had lost the baby.

Imagine him going out in that blizzard after they buried Lizabeth and the baby. He'd come back crippled but ready to take care of his family. One could see that he was fighting his sadness but still trying to be a good father to the rest of the children.

In her mind's eye, Gramma could see Luke and Lizabeth on their wedding day. Lizabeth was tall, blond, her clear blue eyes smiling with the joy of a new bride and the anticipation of a life with Luke. Luke was a bit awkward and ungainly, his dark hair tousled and his suit ill fitting. He wore his work boots because he had no other shoes.

Luke didn't know his heritage. He said his folks were Yankees. Gramma could see his determination, and she respected the way he worked. She knew he would care for a family. Now, Luke moved through life without the spirit he had before.

Gramma couldn't shake off the uneasiness she'd felt when she first heard the owl. Old family folklore had taught her that an owl that hoots in the daytime would bring bad luck.

What had possessed her to come to this god-forsaken wilderness? Here she was, stirring fat for the soap in a big iron kettle. She'd thought that when she'd reached this age she'd be sitting on her porch with Asa, both of them in their rocking chairs, watching their grandchildren play on the grass. Instead, Asa was gone. So were Lizabeth and the baby, and she was caring for her son-in-law and his four children. Was she feeling sorry for herself? Why couldn't she shake off these bad feelings? The children were all well, and, with Luke getting meat, they would have an ample supper. Spring was in the air, and things would be easier.

Ben and Mary were playing with some chips of wood that had fallen when Nathan had split the logs for the day's fire. Maybe later she'd see about making Mary that corn shuck doll she'd been promising her. Back in the fall, she'd put some good shucks on the shelf for it. She'd sit in the sun and let the tiredness bake out of her body while she worked on the doll.

Suddenly, she was seized by a sudden sense of danger. She stood up straight and looked around. "Hurry! Hurry into the cabin!" she cried to the two smaller children, who were at the woodpile. "Don't even stick your noses out 'less I call for you."

She turned to follow them, but in her haste she tripped over a log and fell face first to the ground. As she struggled to get up, she smelled a rank odor. She was too scared to move. The Indian was upon her before she could scream.

"Asa, I'm comin' home to you," she thought. Then, in the next instant, she felt the cold steel of the knife penetrate her body, and she slid slowly to the ground.

CHAPTER THREE

A WHIPPOORWILL SANG

Smoke curled from the chimney of the log cabin, halfway up the hill from the stream where Nathan fished. It had been a hard winter, but now the joyous sounds of spring filled the air. He listened to the whippoorwill singing back there in the woods and another around the bend of the creek. Idly, Nathan wondered what they were doing singing in the daytime. They sounded glad just to be alive.

He leaned back against the sun-warmed rock and thought of how good the sun felt on his shoulders. There hadn't been much to eat since the last big snow. That's when Pa's foot got frostbitten so bad that he couldn't go to hunt until now. He'd been gone since early morning, and Nathan's mouth watered as he thought about the taste of the fresh venison Pa'd be bringing home. A growing boy couldn't fill up right on old potatoes and mush. It was made thin, to stretch out the cornmeal so it would last until they could raise another crop of corn. Pa said they had to save corn for seed, even if they starved a bit.

Nathan watched the corncob bobber float lazily on the water. Fish would help fill his emptiness. He licked his lips and thought about the fish sizzling in the big, black iron skillet. He had carried that heavy iron skillet on his back across the mountains. It would soon be filled with fish, if Nathan had any luck.

Thoughts began to creep into Nathan's mind. He was over a year younger than Sarah, but he felt like he was treated much younger. No, that wasn't right. Sometimes he was treated like a child and other times he was expected to work like an adult. He was a little perturbed with Sarah. She seemed to get all the privileges, even though there weren't many. But she and Gramma had a special relationship, while Nathan and Luke's relationship was distant. He didn't understand his father's aloofness or his background. His father would only say his background was "Yankee." Nathan didn't understand what a Yankee was.

Gramma had sent Sarah into the woods behind the cabin to hunt the new dandelions under the leaves. Nathan's stomach growled as he thought of eating a mess of greens with fish. Maybe there'd even be enough meal so Gramma would fry up some corncakes to go with supper. Maybe that was expecting too much. He'd be satisfied with the fish and the greens.

"I'd better catch that fish 'fore I go to eatin' it," he laughed to himself. He hoped there'd be enough so that he could eat until he couldn't eat another bite. It had been a long time since anyone in the family had a full skin. He didn't see how Gramma kept going. She ate less and less and even gave part of her food to the little ones. She said they needed it to keep up their strength, since they too had the fever that took Ma and the baby. Maybe if they hadn't died, Pa wouldn't have gone off into the woods and got caught in the blizzard and froze his foot. Well, the foot was better now, but it made Pa walk with a slight limp.

Nathan sat up quickly when he saw his bobber go under the water and then pop up again. Something was after the bait. A bite! A good-sized fish was on the line. He waited until the fish was hooked, then he pulled up his pole. It was a keeper and a good start on supper tonight. The whippoorwill sang again as Nathan went to the base of the big oak tree. "He's telling me there's more where that one came from," Nathan chuckled to himself. He crouched behind the tree, looking for the end of a grapevine he could use to string the fish.

As he cut off a good length of it, he felt a prickle of uneasiness that made him shudder. "Somebody's walking across my grave!" He used Gramma's expression. He tried to shrug off the uneasy feeling as he carefully threaded the vine through the gill of the glistening bass. There was the whippoorwill again. It sounded closer to the cabin. The hairs on the back of Nathan's neck rose as he began to bait his hook. "Whee! I've got the whimwhams today!" he thought.

Suddenly, the peace and quiet was shattered by the yelp of the dog. Screams of terror split the air, and the high-pitched gabble of Indians filled his eardrums. He stood for a minute, too shocked to move. There hadn't been any sign of Indians thereabouts for over a year.

He couldn't move. He had to get to the cabin to help Gramma and Mary and little Ben, but his feet seemed rooted to the ground. At last, he grabbed the old gun that Pa had told him to always carry, and he raced up the hill, reaching the clearing just in time to see the cabin burst into flames and an Indian run out the door. In his arms he carried what looked like a bundle of rags. He held it up, and Nathan could see the limpness of it as the Indian carelessly flung it aside. It was one of the children! He could see Gramma lying near the ash hopper.

In his rage, he stumbled into the clearing and fired a shot at the Indian. He missed and stopped to reload. As he knelt, he saw the Indian draw his knife and run toward him. Nathan had no time to reload his weapon but swung it at the Indian, hitting him in the arm so he dropped his knife. Nathan felt the strong arms, like iron bands, wrap around his chest. He felt his breath being squeezed from his body. As he lost consciousness, he realized that what he had heard wasn't a whippoorwill at all.

CHAPTER FOUR

HOGTIED

Nathan was face down in the grass when regained consciousness. He started to get up but found his arms tied behind his back and his legs lashed together. He looked around and saw no one near him. He rolled over on his back.

"Gramma, Gramma," Nathan shouted.

"Gramma, Sarah," he called again.

There was nothing but silence in the forest. The sun shone down on him and all seemed peaceful, except he couldn't move. What would he do now? He tried to sit up but couldn't.

"Gramma, help me. Sarah, where are you?"

He could hear nothing, and fear began to rise up in him. Was he going to die tied up like this? He couldn't walk and could barely crawl on his stomach. He had better inch his way to the cabin.

He was on his stomach, working his way up the hill, when suddenly he was jerked to his feet.

"Whoa, what's happenin' to me?" He said to no one.

The big Indian untied his feet and tied the rawhide strip to his wrists. Then, pointing to the woods, the Indian said, "Come."

Nathan asked, "You mean go?"

"Yes," said the Indian. "Go," as he gestured to another Indian. The second Indian, who stood at the edge of the forest, turned and started into the woods. Nathan had no other choice but to follow the lead Indian. The second Indian kept him reminded that he was a captive by tugging at his bonds. Nathan stumbled along between the pair of braves.

Nathan's embarrassment turned to anger. He was embarrassed because he would be regarded by Luke, Gramma and Sarah as a little kid who couldn't take care of himself and got captured. Gramma and Pa wouldn't say much, but Sarah would be smug. She was into her growth spurt and was taller than Nathan now. Last year they had been the same size. He was getting stronger and broader in the shoulders, but he was younger and shorter. "And now," he thought, "captured by the Indians, as well."

They had pushed through the woods for better than an hour when they stopped to rest.

"Name?" the Indian said to Nathan.

"Nathan. What's your name?"

The Indian didn't answer but said something to the other brave that Nathan didn't understand.

"Nay?" the Indian asked.

"Nathan, Nathan." He replied.

The Indian said something more to the brave, and they started through the forest again.

Nathan watched the brave in front of him. He seemed younger than the Indian who had tied him up. The Indians seemed to be a year or so older than Nathan and weren't hostile to him at all. He seemed to be more interested in tracking through the forest than taking care of Nathan. Maybe he was a young buck learning how to find his way home. The older Indian never gave him directions, as far as Nathan could figure.

"I'm thirsty," Nathan said.

"No water here," the Indian replied.

"Where is the water?" Nathan asked.

"No water here," the Indian said again.

Once again, Nathan's dark thoughts turned inward. Embarrassed, angry, and now he was afraid for his life. Would the Indians kill him? Would he become their slave? How would he escape? Would Pa come a-looking? How did this happen? It started out as a nice, warm, normal spring day. What had happened?

The Indians slowed up and came into a small clearing with a cave off to the side. The Indian motioned for Nathan to sit, and he re-tied Nathan's feet. Nathan's arms hurt from being tied behind his back, and sitting on the ground all tied up was not much better. What would happen next?

CHAPTER FIVE

A MESS OF GREENS

Sarah climbed the steep hill behind the cabin. Her feet shuffled through the limp, damp leaves. In her basket she had yellow-green dandelions, the first of the spring, that she had found hidden under the leaves. They would cook up into a tasty mess of greens to eat with the fish that Nathan was bound to catch. She was hungry. The thought of the roasting meat that Pa would bring from hunting made her cravings even greater.

There'd been little enough food to go around the past winter. Because of the blizzard, Pa's hurt foot had kept him homebound, and the starving animals that were always around the cabin waited for a chance to steal whatever food they could. Well, spring was here, and Pa and Nathan would soon plant corn seed. Pa could hunt again, and there would be berries, and greens in the woods to eat until the corn was ripe. It was good to be alive.

She bent to cut some more dandelions. They were so lacy-looking. It took a good many to fill a pot. It looked as though she had pretty well covered this side of the hill, but she still didn't have enough greens. There had been no sign of Indians for a long time, so she felt safe in going to the other side of the hill. Pa would tan her good if he ever knew that she had wandered so far from the cabin alone. She'd be careful; the lure of finding enough greens so that she could eat until she hurt was more powerful than the fear that Pa might be angry with her. After all, she was certainly able to take care of herself.

The greens on the far side of the hill seemed twice as big as those on the other side of the hill. Quickly, she dropped to her hands and knees and began to cut the tender young shoots. They were so thick in this patch that she soon filled the basket. She stood up and brushed the wet leaves from her knees. Slowly, she picked up her basket and began to walk back home.

The chattering of a squirrel, a sudden whirring sound, and a bright flash of movement startled her so much that she dropped her basket. "Drat! That bird sure gave me a fright!" she thought as she stooped to gather the spilled greens. "I'd better hurry so as not to worry Gramma. No tellin' how long I've been away."

It was much harder going up the hill with a full basket than it was going down. She didn't realize that she had wandered so far. The basket seemed to get heavier and heavier. Would she ever get to the top of the hill? She must have been gone even longer than she thought. It was getting chilly, and she could see the graying sky through the tops of the trees.

The scolding of an angry squirrel startled her. She stumbled over a root, righted herself, and tugged her basket higher on her arm. While she was fourteen, she was still a young girl—and she was much too young to be in the woods by herself. Her faded dress barely had any color left, and her long, thin legs were briar-scratched and mud-streaked. Her bright blue eyes seemed sad, and her blond curls were in need of some attention. Her skirt caught on a branch. With an impatient tug, she tore it loose. Gramma would be angry about that. "Lord knows, it's hard enough to keep up with the cookin' and cleanin' up after you young'uns without me havin' to mend for you, too," she'd chide. "What with your ma gone, and havin' little enough to do with, it plumb wears a body down," Sarah could hear her say.

Gramma had fussed a lot lately about things that didn't count. She never used to be that way. Dimly, Sarah could remember how Gramma had kept up with Ma and Pa on the long trip over the mountains when they came into Kentucky from their old homestead in Pennsylvania. Sarah couldn't remember much about living there. About all she could recall of the journey was being half-hungry all of the time and having Pa carry her over the hard places. That sure had been nice. She thought how she had snuggled her nose in the warm place in his neck, just below where his beard ended. She also remembered Pa telling her that over the next hills was the "Promised Land," where streams ran with milk and honey. "Glory Land," he'd called it. "Well," she said aloud, "There sure ain't been any milk or honey or much of anything else to eat lately. If I don't get home soon, Gramma won't have time to cook these greens today."

The squirrel, nearer now, seemed to be telling her, too, to hurry. There was a clear place ahead, and she could make better time. My, those briars stung. She wished the old squirrel would be quiet. She was beginning to feel uneasy. She knew she had to hurry. He seemed to be fussing at her just like Gramma would when she got back to the cabin. She reached the clearing and began to run. She slipped on some wet leaves and spilled greens from her basket again. There wasn't time to pick them up this time, as she was beginning to panic. She had to get home. Anxiously, she looked behind her as she reached the top of the hill. In a few minutes, she would be safe inside the cabin. The squirrel chattered right in front of her now. Again, she looked back. She turned to run but was stopped in her tracks by the greased, painted body of an Indian. The sound of the chattering squirrel came from his mouth. She screamed only once. The basket fell from her arm and slowly rolled down the hill.

CHAPTER SIX

A LONG WAY TO THE LICKS

Luke had wakened long before daybreak. Carefully, so as not to disturb the sleeping boy on the pallet next to his, he reached for his moccasins. He pulled them on his feet, wincing slightly as the cold leather pulled against the tender skin of the foot that had been frostbitten. It still gave him trouble and would slow him down from the usual pace that he set for himself when hunting. There was no way out of it. He couldn't wait any longer. He'd just have to worry over his slowness and favor the foot. They had to have meat.

Stiffly, he climbed down the ladder. He went to the fire and poked at the black log. On the table lay the food that Gramma had prepared for him to take. He looked over at her in the bed with Sarah. She looked so small; a breeze could blow her away. She was plumb wore out, what with nursing Lizabeth and Beth and the little ones, not to mention himself when he'd come home from the woods with his foot hurting so. She'd been so brave during the hard winter. It was no wonder she was so fretful now.

He remembered that she'd never asked to rest during the long trek over the mountains three years ago, though he could see she was worn to the very marrow of her bones. Hers was the spirit that would make this country great.

He looked at the food on the trestle table he had made. He had built it from a pine tree cleared from the field where the first crop of corn had been grown the first year. Settlers had agreed to raise a crop and build a permanent structure in order to lay claim to the free land.

Luke, with help from Lizabeth, had built the cabin and a makeshift stick-and-mud chimney. The clearing and planting took up most of their time and strength. The next year, he had built a sled. With the help of Nathan, he had hauled rocks on it from the stream and made a good, stone chimney. The stone chimney was the centerpiece of their cabin, and it would last through several lifetimes. He had floored the loft with rough boards for the children to sleep on, and last year he had put a floor in the cabin; Lizabeth was so pleased with having a wooden floor instead of the packed dirt floor.

She had many of Gramma's ways. She liked to keep things tidy. Every day, she sprinkled the floor with sand and swept it clean with her rush broom, so that now the rough places in the boards were worn smooth. He had promised Lizabeth that next year he would build a dog-trot and connect a second cabin to the one in which they lived. The family was growing, and they needed more room. Sarah, Nathan, Ben and Mary were crowded into the loft. Gramma's bed occupied one corner of the cabin, and their bed took up another. There was no room for a cradle, so the baby slept between them. Now that Lizabeth and the baby were dead, what they had would do for the time being.

At this time, he was concerned only about food for the family. Soon, he would have to sow the seed for the corn crop. He remembered how Lizabeth had liked walking behind him dropping corn as he dug the rows. He shrugged off the feeling of loss, even though the pain was severe. He had to concentrate on getting meat for the family, and daylight wasn't far off.

It would be cold in the woods until the sun came up. He took his buckskin shirt off the peg and pulled it over his head. He'd better make tracks so he wouldn't be gone too long. He'd hoped he didn't have to go clear to the licks. He didn't like having to go so far from the place. Things had been peaceful thereabouts for a while, but the settlers never knew when the Indians would rise up and cause trouble.

At the moment, the Shawnees up around a place called Chillicothe had been pretty quiet since Tecumseh had become their leader. Luke didn't feel there was much to worry about as long as he was their chief. Of course, there were always those hostile, renegade bands that would raid and steal anything and everything from unprotected settlers. They were a worry.

On the table he laid the fishhooks he had fashioned for Nathan to use. He should catch some fish today. They would taste mighty good to the family.

Luke slung the shot pouch and powder horn over his shoulder. He put the packet of jerky in the front of his shirt and picked up his rifle. He pulled the heavy door closed behind him. He stood for a moment on the flat rock the children called the stoop and looked around. For some reason, he was slow about getting started this morning.

There was a faint glow of pink in the eastern sky that warned him that he must be on his way. He shrugged off his uneasiness to go and began the loose, steady pace that would enable him to cover miles without becoming tired.

He was alert to everything about him. His eyes moved constantly from one side to the other. Even a bent twig had meaning for him. He could tell from the looks of a track how long it had been since the animal that made it had crossed that place. His were the ways of the woodsman.

He traveled at an even rate until the sun was straight overhead. Only then did he allow himself to stop and rest for a while. He drank from a clear spring and pulled a piece of jerky from his poke. Leaning against a tree, Luke chewed on a piece of stringy meat and let his thoughts wander.

Sometimes he was half sorry they had left the farm in Pennsylvania. He had owned a nice house and good farm land. All his folks and Lizabeth's Pa, Asa, were buried there. They were buried in the old Lutheran churchyard. It was Luke that wanted to move. He wanted more farmland for himself and his growing family. The farm in Pennsylvania was too small to include two sons and maybe some sons-in-law. When he heard the land across the Alleghenies was there for the picking, he decided to go west. He knew that with the sweat of his brow and hard work he could make a farmstead for his family. He knew it would be hard, but the land would be free and clear. Together, he and Lizabeth would make a new home. He had made up his mind.

They sold everything but what they could carry on their backs and pack on the mare. It was hard to part with many of the things they couldn't carry. He remembered Gramma turning her head to hide the tears in her eyes when he took down the clock that had sat on the mantle ever since she and her husband, Asa, had put it there when they first set up housekeeping. Yes, Gramma had grit. He hadn't considered that she would come with them until she announced that she wasn't staying behind, nor was she going back east to live with her brother. She was coming to Kentucky. It was probably the only way she'd ever get to the "Promised Land," she had laughed. Now he didn't know how he'd have made out if it hadn't been for her.

He thought about Sarah. She was beginning to look like her mother and act like her grandmother. That wasn't a bad combination. He shook off his memories.

Time to get moving again. He wanted to get to the salt lick before sundown, when the animals gather there. He was hoping to get a good-sized buck in the morning.

As he neared the lick, he circled around so that he would be downwind from it. Cautiously, he moved closer. He made no sound as he crept through the woods. He waited patiently until three does and a buck came into view. He controlled his breathing and made no movement. He knew that deer couldn't see color, but any movement would spook them. He watched the buck and thought, "Closer, closer."

He knew he had one shot. There would be no time to reload. The deer would be over the next hill before he could reload, and the report from the old muzzle-loader would scare every deer within five miles. He had to be certain. He waited and waited. "Steady," he said to himself.

Now, taking careful aim, he fired the flintlock and dropped the buck. It was a clean kill. He hurried down to the deer and cut his throat to bleed him out.

Swiftly, since it was becoming dark, he slit the carcass, cleaned out the innards, tied a rope to the antlers, and hung the carcass on a branch. He needed to get the deer high enough so predators wouldn't try to get the meat.

Exhausted, he built a fire and stuck strips of liver on the sticks to roast. The liver was very tasty, and Luke knew it wouldn't keep on the trip home. He ate his fill and dropped off into a very heavy sleep.

As soon as it was light enough to see, he cut the deer down the middle so he could fashion two packs that he could carry. He cut a chunk of salt from the lick and added it to the pack. It would help preserve the meat, and the family could always use salt.

It would take him twice as long to get home, since he would have to carry one pack for a ways then leave it hanging from a tree and go back and get the other one. Not only would it take him twice as long but also he would use up twice as much energy. He had made it to the lick in one day. He figured it would take him two days to get back home. That would be a total of three days. It couldn't be helped. He had got the deer. His hungry family could eat well.

He picked up the largest pack after he had tied the other high in the branches of the tree. As he settled the pack securely on his shoulders, he felt uneasy. He looked around. It was almost as though there was someone behind him. "Never had feelings like that before," he said aloud. "Guess I've been living in the past too much lately."

Luke was tired but anxious to get home. It was near the end of the third day since he had left. He didn't have far to go. He had seen no signs of Indians to report to his family. "Guess ole Tecumseh is doin' a good job," he thought as he stepped up his pace. He was eager to see the faces of the children when he showed them the meat. What a feast they would have! Gramma would be fussing around like an old brood hen trying to decide what to cook up first. At last, he'd sit at his own table and watch them eat their fill.

He'd hurry home with this pack and go back first thing in the morning for the other. Maybe he'd even take Nathan with him. It looked quiet enough about so that they could both leave the cabin.

As he started toward the last ridge he could see plumes of smoke rising from the clearing. "Looks like Gramma has the fire going ready for the deer that I'm bringin' in," he thought.

"She's probably got the stew pot out just waitin' to add the meat."

He came over the top of the ridge and stopped dead in his tracks. There before him were the smoking ruins of the cabin. He stood stock still, staring in horror. His mind was unable to comprehend. He stood as though he had turned to stone.

Unnoticed, the pack of meat slid from his shoulders as he dropped to his knees and cried, "No! God, no!"

CHAPTER SEVEN

THE PROMISE

Luke stepped back from the graves he had just dug. Aloud he said, "Lizabeth, you and the baby are not alone. These loved ones have joined you. I failed to protect them and I failed you."

He sat on the stoop, with only the stone chimney rising behind him, put his head down, and sobbed. The ashes were all that was left of the house. He stared at the new graves and tried to speak again but all he could say was, "Lizabeth, I'm sorry."

Slowly, the realization came to him that Nathan and Sarah were not there. Where were they? And why hadn't he thought of them sooner? They might be hiding out in the woods somewhere. He had to find them. He must force himself to think.

The ashes looked to be three days old. The Indians must have raided the day he left. Nathan had been going to fish, so he started toward the stream. Luke was afraid of what he would find. Like a very old, defeated man, he got to his feet. What a fool he was for leaving them! He'd thought they'd be safe, because there hadn't been any trouble from the Indians for so long. Why hadn't he paid more attention to Gramma and her feelings of foreboding? If he had been there, maybe he could have held off the attack. If not, he'd have gone with them. That would have been better than this.

Now he would have to find Nathan and Sarah and do what had to be done. Then he'd leave this place forever. He wished with all his heart that he had never heard of Kentucky.

With dragging steps, he forced himself past the overturned kettle. Slowly, he started across the clearing. He turned his head so as not to see the three new mounds of dirt.

For the first time in his life, he was careless in the woods as he headed toward the stream. He'd even forgotten about his rifle, left where he had dropped it on the hill when he saw the cabin. All he could think about was what he had to do before he could leave.

He reached the rock where Nathan fished. He saw where he had gone to the tree and found the pole leaning against it. There was a grapevine that he used for a stringer with the remains of a fish still attached. There was no sign of Nathan or of a struggle. Then Luke saw the tracks that showed Nathan running toward the clearing. He followed them to the place where Nathan had dropped the gun. It was gone. The ground showed scuffling marks. Hopefully, Luke realized that Nathan might have been taken alive. At least he was alive when he left the clearing. The tracks clearly showed that he had been able to walk. He had not been alone. Shawnee tracks partly covered his. A captive! Nathan had been captured. He might still be alive.

Luke knew that the Indians often took captives for slaves, especially when they were young and healthy, like Nathan. He was almost thirteen years old. It was a good age for the Indians to train him in Indian ways. They took girls, too. But they wanted the girls for their wives. The Shawnee did not object to mixing white blood with theirs. In fact, there were many of them who had French blood running through their veins.

Hope rose in Luke. Maybe Sarah had been captured, too. The life of a slave was miserable, but it was better than no life at all. As the ability to reason returned to Luke, he knew that he had to get his rifle before he could do anything else. He must use every caution because he must save his children. He couldn't help them if he were captured or killed.

He found his rifle where he had dropped it. He went back to the cabin. There was no sign that Sarah had been there when Gramma was attacked. The Indians had disposed of the little ones because they were too much bother to take back. The Indians needed to move quickly, and the babies would have slowed them down. Where was Sarah?

Luke tried to think back to what might have happened to Sarah on the day he left. Normally, Sarah would have been there helping Gramma. She wouldn't have gone far from the cabin. She never went off except to go a little piece into the woods behind the cabin. Usually he or Nathan went with her. Then he remembered Gramma talking about greens. Sarah must have gone to find dandelions to cook with the fish, he decided.

He started through the trees. Soon, he found the place where she had pushed aside leaves and cut the plants. He followed her trail until he came to a bush where a piece of cloth torn from Sarah's dress still hung. A few yards beyond that lay the basket. A trail of wilted greens led him to the place where Sarah had stopped. He saw the moccasin print and knew that Sarah had been captured as well.

Grimly, Luke set his lips. He knew now what he had to do. "Lizabeth, I promise you that I will get them both back safe. I won't fail you again," he vowed aloud. Tears of grief and bitterness streamed down his cheeks.

CHAPTER EIGHT

A MEETING AT THE CAVE

Sarah thought that the Indian would never stop. They had been moving constantly since they left the hill. Her wrists hurt where the rawhide thong cut into her flesh as he pulled her along. When she stumbled, he'd jerk the strap until it felt as though her arms would be yanked clear off her body. The bushes slapped and clawed at her. At first, she had been too scared to even notice them. Now her body felt like one big welt. She tried to avoid the sharp stings, but she couldn't always see the branches in time.

She kept her eyes fastened on the brown figure ahead of her who kept her at such a constant pace. The Indian wore only a breechcloth, and his coarse, black hair was parted down the middle and tied on each side with strings of deer hide just below his ears. She could smell that his body had been greased with bear fat. It was a very pungent odor. It wasn't fresh bear fat either, she thought.

As though the savage could read her mind and didn't like her thoughts, he jerked the line to make the girl move faster.

"I'll show him!" she thought as she stumbled along after him. The Indian moved soundlessly through the underbrush. Sarah made as much noise as though she were driving cattle.

They kept on traveling until mid-afternoon when they reached a small cave near the stream they had followed for some time. The Indian pushed Sarah into the cave and tied the thong to a rock that jutted out from the wall.

The Indian glared at Sarah and said, "Stay." Ducking his head at the entrance, he went out. Sarah was so tired that she lay down where she had fallen. She hardly noticed that he had gone. After she had rested, she began to think. What would Gramma do when Sarah didn't come home? She would be very worried. She wouldn't know that Sarah had been so foolish and gone so far from the cabin. Poor Gramma. She'd be half out of her mind with worry. How could she know there had been an Indian in the woods?

Sarah began to wonder where the Indian had gone. Afraid to be with him, she was more afraid to be alone. Suppose he'd gone off and left her tied to the rock? Maybe some wild animal would get her, or she might starve. She didn't like the way the Indian looked, or the way he smelled, or the way he had pulled her along, but she wished he would come back.

What she really wished was that Pa'd walk though that opening. Pa! What would he say when he found out that she had disobeyed Gramma and gone to the other side of the big hill? He'd sure be upset with her for not doing what she was told. Why had she been so greedy for more greens?

Greens! Sarah wished she had some now. She was so hungry she could eat them raw. "I wonder how many fish Nathan caught," she pondered.

Her stomach growled with emptiness. It seemed that she could smell the fish cooking right now. When she shut her eyes and thought about the crisp skin and flaky white meat of the fish, she could almost taste it. Maybe if she kept her eyes shut, she could pretend she was eating fish. The smell was even stronger. It was almost as though the fish were right in front of her. Sarah sighed and rolled over. It was no use pretending. It just made her hungrier. As tired as she was, she fell into a deep sleep.

"Don't!" Sarah muttered as she felt her shoulder being shaken, "Let me be. I'm too tired to get up yet, Gramma."

Slowly, she began to waken. It was cold and she was hungry. She was still in the cave. Being home had been a dream. Still, she smelled cooked fish. Unwillingly, Sarah opened her eyes. She blinked. Surely, this, too, was a dream. She couldn't believe her eyes. There before her on the floor of the cave was a steaming, fresh-cooked fish. With grimy hands, the starving girl snatched at it, pulled off a large chunk and stuffed it into her mouth. Never had anything tasted so good. Sarah tore at the fish until there was nothing left of it. Finally, she sat back and wiped her hands on her torn skirt. Only then did she notice that she was no longer tied.

Awareness came back to her, and she realized that the Indian must have untied her while he caught the fish and then cooked it. He was not going to let her starve, after all. It certainly made her feel better since she had eaten. Now she must think. Never had she been so frightened that she was unable to think. What could she do? Escape! Pa would escape. Then so would she.

The entrance of the cave was ahead of her. She jumped to her feet and started toward it. Somehow she would find her way home.

Just as she reached the opening, it darkened. The big body of the Indian blocked out the light and stopped her from going any farther. From behind him, she heard the guttural voices of other Indians. As she slipped to the ground, into unconsciousness, she heard her name being called.

CHAPTER NINE

ANOTHER PROMISE

"Sarah! Sarah! Wake up!!" She was being shaken so hard that her head rolled from side to side. She didn't want to wake up. She wanted to stay in the safe darkness that held no Indians, no terror. The voice wouldn't let her be. "Sarah! Sarah!" It was pulling her back to consciousness. Dimly she realized that it was a voice she knew.

A smart slap across her cheek stung her. "Don't hurt me," she said weakly and began to cry.

"Sarah! Sarah! You must wake up!" Lightly she was slapped again.

Nathan! Nathan! It was Nathan! What was he doing here? Now fully awake, she sat up quickly.

"Did you come to save me, Nathan? How did you ever find me? Did Gramma send you? Is she very put out with me for wandering so far? I guess she was really worried when I didn't come back. Oh, Nathan, I am so glad you found me!" Sarah was so happy to see Nathan that she chattered on without thinking. Suddenly she stopped talking as she realized that they were still in the cave. She didn't like being there.

"Sarah, are you all right? The Indians didn't hurt you, did they?" he asked.

"No, only my legs and arms sting where the bushes scratched me. We went so fast that I had a stitch in my side, but that's gone now. Did Gramma send you after me? Was she awful mad at me? I 'spect she was half out of her mind when I didn't come home. Poor Gramma," she sighed.

"Sarah, listen to me," Nathan put up his hand to stop her talking.

She raised her head and looked him full in the face. She opened her mouth to speak again but stopped before a sound came out. Her eyes opened wider and wider as she heard voices outside the cave. They said Indian words. Then she knew that Nathan, too, had been captured.

Her shoulders slumped. Without knowing what she was doing, she began pulling threads from the torn place on her dress and rolling them into tight little balls between her fingers. She didn't want to think. Nathan was talking to her, but she didn't want to listen.

Finally some of his words pierced her unwillingness. "Ben! Mary! Fire! Gramma!" What was he saying? She began to listen as Nathan told her about the Indian raid on the cabin. Nathan wasn't sure but he thought that Gamma and one of the little children might have been hurt or worse. He didn't know what happened to the other child. The cabin was on fire.

Tears of worry and anger rolled down her cheeks as she heard what might have happened to Gramma and the little children. "What would Pa find when he got home and they were all gone?" she asked herself.

"Sarah," Nathan got her attention again. "We've got to make a plan. We've got to get back to Pa."

"Escape! Nathan was thinking just like Pa," she thought. She wiped her grimy face with the hem of her dress. "What can we do? How can we get away?" she asked.

"I don't know yet. All I know is these Indians are Shawnee so we are lucky. Shawnees don't torture prisoners. Shooting Star is the big chief. Think Pa said his name was Tecumseh. Pa says he's a good Indian as Indians go. He's tryin' to help his people."

"Humph!" Sarah snorted. "Gramma says that the only good Indian is a dead 'un. From the way they smell, I'd say that she's right."

"Sarah, you watch your mouth. Some of these Indians know a little English. You don't want to make them mad at us. Besides, there are many good Indians around. You keep your feelings to yourself and don't go spoutin' off about anything like you was at home." Nathan cautioned her.

He silenced her for a while and she sat thinking. "What do you think they'll do with us?" She was beginning to be afraid again. There was no telling what the Indians had planned. Well, for one thing, they won't do anything until daylight. They ain't movin' at night. It ain't their nature.

"At daylight, what then?" Sarah interrupted. Now she didn't want to think of leaving the comfort of the cave.

Nathan thought for a while. Finally, he said, "It's my guess they'll take us to one of their camps. They'll probably make us slaves. You'll live in one of the quonsets and work for the wives. They will give you all the jobs they don't want to do, and they will teach you their ways. Then a brave will select you as a wife and . . ."

Nathan got no farther. "One of his wives?" Sarah gasped. "Marry! I'd rather die first."

"Shhh! Sarah! I told you to watch your mouth. That ain't goin' to happen. We're goin' to get away. And don't tempt an Indian to kill ya, 'cause they will."

"But how will we escape?"

"I don't know yet. Let me study on it. We'd better get some sleep. No tellin' how far they'll travel tomorrow. We need rest."

"Nathan, I'm powerful scared." Sarah murmured as she lay down on the hard rock floor of the cave. "I want to go home."

"I'm here, Sarah. I'll take care of you as best I can." Nathan lay down beside her and put his arm over her.

Like the two tired children they were, they quickly dropped off into a deep sleep.

In his sleep, Nathan muttered, "I'll take care of you, Sarah, I will."

At sun-up they were awakened by moccasined feet poking at them. Grunting and pointing, the Indians showed them they were heading north. The savage who had captured Sarah picked up the thong and tied it around her wrists. She pulled back as he picked up the other end of it. "Go now," the Indian said.

Then he grinned at the other Indians and boasted proudly, "This one, she mine," as he started off into the forest pulling Sarah as he went.

Again, Sarah became overwhelmed with fear as she stumbled after him. She begged half out loud, "Oh, God, please help me."

CHAPTER TEN

A CALL FOR HELP

Luke stumbled into the stockade. His eyes were feverish and he swayed with fatigue. "Indians!" he cried hoarsely. "Indians!"

Quickly, a crowd gathered around him. "Indians!" the word spread like wildfire through the camp. There'd been no sign of Indians for so long that the people had begun to feel safe. They had become careless. Now mothers gathered their children close to them and men looked to their rifles. Uneasiness hung over all of them.

Most of the people at the fort were newly arrived in Kentucky. They had been lured here by the essays of men like Gilbert Imlay and Bernard Mayo, who wrote stories of the beauty of the land and how it was called *"The Goshen of the West."* The newer arrivals hadn't yet felt the threat of the Indians, who resented the white man coming into their land and plowing up their hunting grounds. Now, settlers were forced to face the Indian resentment. A cabin had been raided. A woman and two children were dead. Two other children were kidnapped. Fear was in the air.

The men moved closer to their families. Soon, they planned to leave the safety of the fort. They planned to go into the wilderness to homestead land, build their cabins and clear the land. They would be leaving the protection of the garrison at the fort and going off alone. They worried about leaving their wives and children alone, as they would have to hunt for meat and go for supplies. This tragedy could happen to them, too.

A big man pushed his way through the crowd around Luke. "What's this about an attack?" he asked. "There ain't been no Indian sign since the winter before last."

With pain, Luke began to tell his story. When he got to the part where the signs showed that Sarah had been captured, he completely broke down. His children were out there somewhere, prisoners of the Indians. "No tellin' what's happened to them," he sobbed.

"What tribe were they, Luke?" one man asked.

"Looked to be Shawnees. Could be it's a renegade group or maybe another tribe tryin' to look Shawnee. Don't ever really know with Indians. I just pray it *is* Shawnees. They're more decent than other Indians around. If it's Shawnee, they'll be headin' north to one of their settlements on the big river, or they may be goin' to a place they call Chillicothe. I don't rightly know. All I know is that all signs point north. I'll go alone for my young'uns if I have to, but I'd sure appreciate some help in gettin' 'em back. I know Nathan and Sarah are with the Indians. Don't know if they'll end up at the same place or not. Gramma and the two little ones are gone. Guess the Indians figured Gramma was too old and slow and the little ones too much of a bother to make the trip. Looks to me like the Indians are goin' a long way; otherwise they would have taken the two little ones." Luke reasoned.

"How far did you follow the trail?" Sam Stewart asked.

"I went up to where the stream forks over the ridge four, five miles from here when I followed Nathan's trail. On Sarah's, they went toward the main rise. They went in two different ways. Had to be the same tribe, but don't know if they'll end up in the same village. That's why I need help. Time's a wastin' and I can't go two ways at once."

A trapper, Sam'l, stepped forward. "I'm with you, Luke," he said. "How many men do you reckon you'll need?"

"Two or three for each trail," Luke replied. "No men who are green to this country. Just men who can read signs and know the Indian ways."

Several men stepped forward. Luke considered them. "John, you're a good man, and I know what you are thinkin', but you ain't been here long enough to know what the signs say. You're needed at the fort in case there's a full-scale attack. You're a good shot with the rifle. Sam'l, you come along. You ain't got chick nor child to fret after you if you get took. Squire, you know more about Indian ways than any man here. I'll need you. Jason, you got the grit we need to hold to the trail. You can go longer on less than any man I've ever seen. James, I can't ask you. You've got the responsibility of the whole stockade on you. You need to be here. Lige, you can read trail better than any man I've ever hunted with. Matthew, you're the best stalker in a close place I know." One by one, Luke chose the men who would help get his children back.

There was no need to talk. Each man was a veteran of the woods. He knew what he would need and what he would have to do. Swiftly, they prepared to leave the fort. In complete unspoken agreement, they divided themselves into groups of three. Squire was acknowledged leader of one, Luke the second. Jason and Sam'l lined up with Squire, while Matthew and Lige followed Luke.

The heavy, log gate of the fort slowly swung closed behind the men. Inside, preparations were being made in case of an

Indian attack. The easy-going ways were gone; each person was anxious and alert. The Indians might never come, but in case they did, the people in the fort would be ready.

The six men entered the forest, each with his own thoughts and a dedicated spirit to get the children back.

CHAPTER ELEVEN

TWO TRAILS MEET

"Looks like they stopped here for the night, Jason. These ashes in the clearing have been cold three, four days at the most. The prints around here are the same tracks we've been seeing. Some of them are pretty scuffled, like they pow-wowed here."

"They must have spent some time here. They've been in the cave. Can't tell much about it in the dusk."

"Squire, come out of that cave and look over here. 'Pears to be another set of tracks coming in from this way."

"Yep, Sam'l. These are different from them of the Indians we've been following that took the boy."

The three men examined the trail for a short way into the woods. "Looks like just one Indian on this trail, and he had the girl. They must have planned to meet here. Luke's party should be showin' up soon, since he's on the girl's trail. That Indian sure took the long way 'round to get here."

"Funny thing, they didn't bother to cover their tracks around here. The trail was hard enough to follow from Luke's place up 'til now. Here, a baby could read the signs."

"Guess they didn't expect to be followed so soon. They probably watched the cabin before they raided and saw Luke goin' off to hunt. Indians smart as Shawnees usually study out a place before they hit it."

"They must have only gone to Luke's place, small band like this. Looks to be just five of them, from the tracks. Could be renegades, Jason."

"Could be they're meetin' up with a war party, too." Sam'l studied the tracks again.

"Yep! Might be there's raidin' parties at other outlyin' cabins like Luke's. I heard that the Shawnee had some kind of fever sickness that killed off a bunch of them. Mostly children. They might be gettin' young'uns to keep up the tribe number. They get 'em young as these of Luke's and they can pretty well train them in the Indian ways. Pretty soon the boys and girls begin thinkin' they're Shawnees instead of . . ." Squire suddenly stopped talking and raised his rifle ready to shoot.

There had been no noticeable sound from the forest, but he sensed something was there.

Silently, the men slipped to find cover. They watched as the bushes were cautiously parted. Three men came into view; Matthew and Lige closely followed by Luke stepped into the clearing. Squire walked out to meet them.

With a few words, he told Luke about finding the sets of tracks that met. Luke sighed with relief. He knew that at least Nathan and Sarah were together. They could comfort each other. It would be easier, too, just having one trail to follow. In the morning, they could start tracking again. It was too late in the day now to see well enough to read the signs.

"Ain't no need for all of us to go on," he decided. "Sam'l, if you'll come with me, the others can go back to the fort. We'll stir up a lot less fuss in the woods and can get there faster if we ain't an army."

The men accepted what he said as being practical. At daybreak they parted.

No one wished Luke and Sam'l luck. They would either rescue the children or be killed or captured themselves. All frontiersmen understood this.

CHAPTER TWELVE

LIFE IN THE VILLAGE

Sarah was terrified by the number of Indian women who gathered around her as she was shoved into the light of a huge bonfire. They poked at her with stiff fingers and grunted as they did so. They felt her blond hair and tried pulling it. She tried to stay beside Nathan, but he was soon led away. Bravely, she tried to keep back tears of rage and frustration. She stood straight and tall and held her head high. She was taller than most Indian women. If only she could rest and clean up, she could endure whatever they had in mind for her.

An older woman approached her. She scattered the women like so many chickens, and, taking Sarah not un-gently by the arm, led her to a smaller fire. There, with a gesture, she indicated that Sarah should sit on the ground. A stick hung over the fire. Spitted on it was a half-cooled animal of some sort. The Indian woman reached toward it with her hand and pulled off a piece of meat. She handed the meat to Sarah.

Sarah didn't even notice that the hand that held the meat was still unwashed from the time it had skinned that same animal. Ravenously, she pulled and tugged at the meat with her

53

teeth while juices from it ran down her chin and stained her dirty, torn dress.

She also didn't notice that the woman had gone into the shelter they sat in front of. She returned, carrying a gourd of an astringent smelling salve. She set the gourd on the ground near Sarah.

Finally, Sarah had satisfied her hunger enough to look around. Everyone seemed busy at some task or other. There were many shelters like the one behind her, and many people seemed to belong to each shelter. Sarah was too tired to wonder much about what was happening. She slid into a curled position and cradled her head on her arms. Sleep would not be held off. Soon, a moccasin toe nudged her from slumber. She struggled to wake up. Finally, she sat up to find that the woman was handing her the gourd that contained the salve. She pointed to the salve and then to Sarah's cuts and scratches. All Sarah wanted to do was sleep. However, the woman would not leave her alone until she had smeared salve on the places that were cut. At last, having satisfied the woman's urgings, Sarah was allowed to go to sleep.

At daybreak, Sarah's arm was roughly shaken. Reluctantly, she opened her eyes to find that she was inside the hut, sleeping on a pallet of rough furs. A young woman was standing over her. Impatiently, by gestures, she indicated that Sarah was to come with her. Sore and bruised, Sarah slowly got to her feet and limped outside. The young woman attached a leather thong to one of Sarah's still raw and bleeding arms and led her to the edge of the woods. There she heaped Sarah's arms high with firewood and led her back to the camp. After several trips back and forth, Sarah was given a bone with some meat left on it. It looked like something that should have been thrown to the dogs. Sarah didn't notice. She was too hungry to care. When the meat had been eaten off the bone, Sarah was still hungry, and like a dog, she gnawed at the bone, hoping to find a shred of meat or marrow she had missed.

All day, she was led back and forth until the pile of wood she had carried was higher than she could reach. At nightfall, she was too tired to even wonder what had happened to Nathan.

Later the next day she saw him. He was with some young braves who had just come in from the hunt. She hardly recognized him, as he was covered with blood. She ran to where he stood. At his feet was a pile of small animals. His eyes met hers but warned her to say nothing. Instead, he pointed to the game and said, "Girl, skin these for your family. Come pick them up and take them to your house."

When she got close enough to hear a whisper, he said, "I'm fine, Sarah. They're takin' me on hunts. I carry back what they kill. I'm watchin' an' waitin'. If I get a chance, I'll get you away from here. Do whatever you are told. Learn everything you can about the ways of the Indians. Now go! Don't look back."

Sarah gathered the squirrels and rabbits and carried them back to the old woman, who indicated that Sarah was to skin and clean the animals. Later, she roasted them over the open fire. There was plenty of meat to eat now, but oh, how she wished for some vegetables. Perhaps she could find some greens in the woods. The fiddleneck ferns should be up by now. Maybe tomorrow, she thought, she would get a chance to look for some when she was gathering wood.

Her thoughts were interrupted by the arrival of several braves to the camp. This meant that, as a slave, Sarah would be worked much harder than usual. The men would talk far into the night, and she would have to serve them if they became thirsty or hungry. She sighed and began to build up the fire to prepare the meal for them.

The woman, Little Bird, called her from the fire. For some reason Sarah did not understand, Little Bird seemed to like

Sarah. She had given Sarah salve, and now she handed Sarah several deerskins. By signs, she told Sarah that she was to make herself clothing from them.

Sarah was grateful. The clothes she had worn were tattered and filthy. Now, with help from Little Bird, she could make herself an outfit that would make her feel more like a person. At least she would be clean and wouldn't stand out as she did as a blond-haired, blue-eyed girl wearing a tattered dress. She promised herself that she would find a way to bathe before she wore any of the new clothing.

As the days passed, Sarah was given more and more freedom and more and more responsibility. She wore her outfit of skins and became more comfortable wearing it. Soon she was allowed to go to the river alone to get water in the birch pails that she had learned to make. Sarah was grateful because each time she went to the river she washed her face and hands. She was as content as she could be as a slave. She had food, decent clothing, and was as clean as she could keep herself. She had learned many useful things.

She watched Nathan for signs that he had a plan. He was often gone all day with hunting parties. He had gained the confidence of the Indians to the degree that he carried a small bow and was learning to shoot arrows from it. The young Indian boys were trained to hit a target with their first arrow. At first, they had laughed at Nathan's clumsiness, but now he could hit a running rabbit or squirrel with an arrow half of the times he shot.

He learned to move through the forest without making a sound. He left scarcely any trail to be followed. Being with the Indians sharpened those skills he had learned from Pa. His life depended on his abilities. Indians had no use for anyone who could not be useful to them or be respected by them. Nathan learned as quickly as he could. He still wanted to escape and return to Pa, but he thought that if they didn't escape, life wouldn't be so bad. He enjoyed hunting with the men and learning how to track the animals they needed. Like Pa, they only killed those they could use for food. Even the skins became clothing. Nothing was wasted.

Much of the smaller game they brought back to camp had been caught and skinned by Nathan. He was usually a bloody mess after skinning the animals. He didn't bother to wash afterward. No one cared whether he bathed or not. He could easily live with that.

Nathan knew that girls grow up quickly in the wilderness. Before long, Sarah would be considered by the Indians old enough to become a wife. He knew that they must get away before that happened or it never would. He had learned that the festival for choosing of the brides was to be soon. To prepare for the feasting of the occasion, all of the braves—and those they trusted--would bring in much meat. They would hunt daily. It was a good excuse for Nathan to make many arrows. He hoped that he would have some left for when he could manage the escape. They would get away or they would die. Nathan would make sure that no matter what happened he would save one arrow to make sure that Sarah was not captured again. Failing to escape would not be pleasant, especially for a girl. Indians had ways of showing their displeasure in ways that were too terrifying for Nathan to think about. One way or the other, he would save his sister.

CHAPTER THIRTEEN

A GOOD HUNT

Sarah's arms were piled high with wood. She didn't know how much wood she had carried that day. It seemed like a whole forest. With a clatter, she let the last logs fall on the ground. The woman who was stirring the meat in a big kettle dropped her paddle and yelled at Sarah.

"I wouldn't even care if she hit me," thought Sarah. "I'm just too tired to care."

She crept around to the back of the bark-covered quonset in which she slept and, feeling grateful, sat down on the hard ground. When she had rested for a while, she thought about their captivity. Several other captives were in the camp when she and Nathan had arrived. Three more were brought in yesterday. None of them had been hurt by the Indians.

It wasn't as bad in the village as she had feared. Most of the women were very kind to each other and to the children. All of the children seemed warm and loving to Sarah. She had as much to eat as anyone; in fact, she had more to eat now than she did at home. The Shawnees were good hunters and brought back plenty of game for the women to clean and cook. That meant plenty of skins that Sarah had to help cure. She didn't like having to scrape the hairs off the hides that were stretched on willow racks. She used a sharp stone as a scraper. Her hands were becoming calloused from the rock pressing in the same places on her palms.

Grinding the corn to make meal was something that she liked to do. She could sit by the big, hollowed-out rock and rub the dry kernels with a smaller stone until they looked like gold dust in the sun. The rhythm of the movement pleased her, and the sun felt good on her back. The corn smelled so clean and good—it was about the only thing in the village that did.

Never would she get used to the other smells. She even went out of her way to avoid the rocks where the fish were dried. She hated having to go into the quonset, where the odor of bear grease and unwashed bodies seemed so much stronger than in the open air. Sarah tried to keep herself as clean as she could. She was beginning to look like an Indian, but she was not going to smell like one if she could help it.

Being out in the sun so much had tanned her skin and turned her hair a coppery gold color. The only thing that distinguished her from the Indian girls was her blond hair and blue eyes. She wore her hair in a braid that hung down her back. The end of the braid was tied with a piece of rawhide thong. It was like the rawhide that the Indian had used to tie her wrists. She would always have scars on her wrists where the leather strap cut into her flesh.

The Indians did not mistreat her. They worked her hard enough, but Sarah didn't mind that too much. She was used to working hard. Gramma had always kept her busy. "The devil finds work for empty hands," Gramma would say and set Sarah on another task as soon as she had finished what she was doing.

The girl fought off a feeling of homesickness when she thought about Gramma. At least Nathan was in the same village with her, though she didn't see him often. They had tried to get alone and make a plan to escape, but so far they hadn't come up with one they thought would work.

Today, she hadn't seen Nathan at all. He had been taken along with the hunting party that had gone out soon as it was light. Of course, he wasn't trusted with a rifle. There were only two or three rifles in the village, and they were property of the biggest chiefs. One of those was the old muzzle-loader that belonged to Nathan when he was captured.

Nathan was strong and wiry for an almost thirteen year old. His job was to carry back the game that was killed. "Nathan sure would be a mess when he got back and stinkin' with the smell of animals he had carried," Sarah thought. "He'd smell as bad as the others."

For once she was glad that he slept in another shelter. She was thankful that she wouldn't have to smell him, too. Tonight she'd put the skins she slept on just as close to the opening of the quonset as she dared. The smells didn't seem to bother the Indian women, but they made Sarah's stomach heave.

The Indian women were excited about something. The women chattered constantly and were impatient with her slowness more than they had been when she first arrived. Sarah hadn't been a captive long enough to understand the strange, guttural language that they used. She hoped she wouldn't be in the village long enough to learn it, either. Though she did wish that she understood enough to know what was causing the whole camp to be in an uproar.

She'd better get back to the campfire before she was missed. The women left her pretty much alone, but if she were gone too long, they'd come looking for her. She'd kept this quiet place in the forest to herself and didn't want to be found here. It was the only place in the camp that she thought of as especially hers. Here, she felt like Sarah again instead of just a slave to an Indian woman.

She went for another armload of wood to carry to the fire. As she straightened up from dropping wood, she noticed that the hunting party was coming back. Sarah hurried over to join the women. She would have to help work on the meat. Loudly, the women grunted about the fine hunt, pleased with what the men laid before them.

Sarah took a step back as a young buck was placed at her feet. Startled, she looked up, and her eyes met those of the Indian who had captured her. What did he want, she wondered?

"Big feast," he said. "Many braves come. Pick wives."

There weren't many unmarried women in the village. There were several girls her age and a little older. She knew that the Indian girls were married young and taken to the quonset of the brave's family to care for her man's needs. Two young wives lived in the same shelter that Sarah did.

She looked at the buck lying before her. The Indian's feet were almost touching it. Puzzled, she looked at him again.

He grinned down at her. Waves of fear washed through her body. Terrified, she turned and ran.

CHAPTER FOURTEEN

A PLAN IS MADE

Luke and Sam'l had been lying on the bluff above the Indian settlement since long before dawn. They were carefully hidden from the view of anyone looking up. For many weeks, they had watched the activity below and studied the habits of the Indians. Luke was impatient with the delay, but he knew that before they could act to free Sarah and Nathan it would be wise to know as much as possible. He was satisfied that the children were unharmed. Many times during the day, he would see Sarah moving about the camp. It seemed to Luke that she was being treated better than he had expected. She was worked hard, but not harder than she could bear.

Until today, the rescue party had seen Nathan only in the morning when he left with the hunting parties and again when they returned with the meat they had killed. No hunters went out today. They could see Nathan helping to burn out a log that was to become a dugout canoe. They had seen several other children who were not Indian in the village. Luke wondered what other families had been raided and how many had been taken to other places.

He noticed that Sarah didn't appear to be watched too closely by the women. They had all seemed to be too busy to pay much attention to what she was doing. Several times she had gone alone to the river for water.

Luke stopped chewing on a piece of jerky and watched as several braves he had not seen before came around the bend of the river. They were not painted. They had come in peace. The canoes they paddled were made of birch bark, not the hollowed out, shaped logs that were used by the Indians of the village. They must have come from farther north where birch canoes were more common. There was excitement in the camp over their coming. These braves must have been expected.

Slowly, Sam'l turned his head to look at Luke. There was a question in his eyes. Luke arched his eyebrows to show that he, too, was puzzled about the happenings. Something was in the air. There was no doubt about that, what with the bringing in of more meat than was needed and the bustle of the women. Might be a ceremony of some sort. They'd have to be patient until they knew what was happening.

"Wonder if Luke has made a plan yet? I'd rather walk a week without stoppin' than spy on some Redskins," Sam'l thought. Even though Sam'l was much younger than Luke, he was cramped from lying still so long. He would be glad when they could take some kind of action. He knew that what they were doing was the best thing, but that didn't mean he had to like it.

Luke had studied the way the bluff ran. With care, he could crawl down behind some bushes and reach the river. It was risky, but it was the only way he could think of to let Sarah know he was there. If he failed, Sam'l could go back for help. He'd watch for his chance. He signaled Sam'l what he planned to do. Now, he must force himself to wait for the best time to start. The warm sun was directly overhead when Luke saw that a huge fire was being built in front of the council house. Women were carrying great chunks of meat and putting them on spits.

Everyone in the village seemed to be busy, and the sound of the activity reached the watchers on the bluff. It was time to move. Carefully, Luke wormed his way on his stomach to a clump of bushes near the water. He wanted to get closer to where Sarah usually went, but there was nothing large enough to hide him. He'd just have to wait here and hope to get her attention. He hoped that it would be Sarah who was sent for water. He watched as best he could without showing himself.

It seemed to him that it was hours before he heard someone coming. With great care, he raised himself to see who it was. His heart seemed to stop. It was Sarah, and she was alone. He wanted to jump out, grab her and run, but he knew that would be foolish. He must get her attention. He picked up a pebble that lay on the ground by his knee and lightly tossed it toward Sarah. Startled, she looked up and started to turn. "Don't look around! Keep on doin' what you're doin'! Don't turn!" he whispered to her as softly as he could. "Don't talk! Listen!"

She stood as though frozen. She couldn't believe her ears. Pa! It was Pa! How did he get here? How did he find her? Tears rolled down her cheeks.

"Come closer, but stay at the river. Slowly now. Act natural."

As though in a trance, she obeyed. She didn't believe that she wasn't dreaming.

"Sarah, find Nathan. Tell him when the feast is goin' strong he's to slip away to the river. He should go round through the woods to the dugouts and lay down inside the closest one to this bush. You count—slow—to a hundred when you see him leave. Then come down, like you been doin', to get water. Get in the dugout with Nathan. Remember, don't let anybody hear you talk to him. If you understand, take some water in your hands, like you was washin' your face."

Slowly, she bent over. She put both hands in the cool water and splashed it on her face. It was real! She wasn't dreaming! She washed her face again to be sure.

"Now go back up. Be careful to act like always, or you'll give yourself away." He wanted to turn and watch her go, but he didn't dare. He'd chanced too much already. Everything depended on Sarah. He prayed that she could carry it off. He dreaded the thought of what would happen if she didn't.

CHAPTER FIFTEEN

CELEBRATION

Everyone in the village was gathered around the huge fire. It would be a great feast. The women chattered constantly as they stirred the stew and turned the spits. The young unmarried braves were still in the council house with the chiefs. The other men sat quietly and waited for them to come out. Many brave and tried warriors were in the village. They had been arriving throughout the afternoon. Most of them had come by way of the river. Their canoes were clustered closely together at the water's edge. Little Bird stood in the door of the quonset. They were ready to begin. They had much to celebrate tonight: the successful hunt, the many slaves taken in the raids, and the choosing of the brides. It was the choosing of the brides that had Sarah very worried.

A silence fell upon the Indians as the chief, Brave Wolf, stepped to the door of the quonset. Many strings of wampum hung around his neck. He was a great warrior who had counted much coup. Respectfully, they waited for his signal to begin the ceremony. With dignity, he raised his arm and looked over the people before him. It was good. He began to speak. He called upon the Great Spirit to see how strong the warriors were and what great hunters they were, also. He told of the many deer that had been killed. He named Red Arrow as the man who killed more deer than any other hunter. He told of the raids and named each man who had brought in a captive. He spoke for many minutes on what had been done. Finally, he named the warriors who could take a wife that night. As he named them, he told of each man's achievements. Each in turn, the brave of whom he spoke stood forward. The last was Running Deer, who had captured Sarah.

On the edge of the crowd, Sarah again felt fear when she saw him standing at the council house. She knew that she didn't dare run. That would call attention to her. She forced herself to stand unmoving through the speeches of the other chiefs. It seemed to her that hours went by before they stopped.

Each chief talked about the raids, the captives, the hunting. They said much the same thing that Brave Wolf had said. The Indians listened respectfully, as though they had never heard it before. They grunted agreement at each feat that was mentioned. It was the right of each man to be heard, they believed, and so the speeches went on until the last chief had spoken.

Again, Brave Wolf stood and raised his arm. "Let the feast begin," he called in a loud voice. As he dropped his arm, whoops and yells filled the air.

Sarah thought her head would split with the noise. The feasting and dancing began. Sarah was kept so busy helping the women serve the men that for a while she almost forgot where she was. She had managed to see Nathan earlier and had signaled him that she must speak to him. It had been too risky then. There were many people around. Now she was worried that she would not be able to find him in this crowd. As a slave, he was not seated with the men, and she was constantly being called by one or another woman to do something. She wished she could see Nathan.

Little Bird sent Sarah to stir the stew at the cooking fire. She could hardly see for the smoke that was coming from under the kettle. Someone must have put green logs on the flames. She hoped Little Bird wouldn't blame her for it. Her eyes stung from the smoke.

"Sarah! Sarah!" the whisper came from the edge of the woods. "Come over here, I made the fire smoke so they wouldn't see us talking. Hurry! I can't be gone long."

Sarah dropped the stirring paddle and ran toward Nathan's voice. "Nathan, only listen, don't talk." Quickly, she told him what Pa had said for him to do.

"You be where I can see you, or I won't know you're gone," she finished.

"It'll be about an hour before I can get loose from what I've got to do. Start watchin' then. I'll try to be on this side of the big bonfire. Now get back to your stirrin'; that woman is comin' this way."

By the time Little Bird reached the stew kettle, Sarah was stirring like she'd never been gone. Angry, Little Bird grunted at Sarah and pushed her aside. She bent and, fussing at Sarah, pulled the green log from the fire. Sarah didn't care what Little Bird thought or did. Her heart was pounding. Pa was here. He'd save them from the Indians. They'd be free in just a little while. She scooped up some of the stew and began to eat. It was best to have food inside her before they left. No telling when they'd be able to eat again. She wished she could take some for Pa, but that would be too dangerous. She must be very careful. Lost in her thoughts, she didn't notice that someone had come between her and the fire. When she finished the last of the stew, she licked her fingers clean and wiped them on the weeds. She would like to have washed her hands, but she couldn't go to the river until Nathan left.

She better get back to the stew and stir a while. She stood up and realized that she was not alone. Looking up, she saw Running Deer grinning at her as though he knew a secret. She felt as though her heart would stop. She gasped, turned and ran as fast as she could to the circle of women.

CHAPTER SIXTEEN

WALK SLOWLY

Sarah stayed as close as she could to the women. Impatiently, she waited for Nathan to come to where she could see him. Time had never passed so slowly for her. She was more afraid now than ever of Running Deer and wanted to be as far away from him as she could get.

The Indians were dancing around the fire. As they danced, their excitement grew and the dance became more and more wild. Sarah prayed that Nathan would hurry. She couldn't bear to wait much longer.

She tried to look as busy as possible so that she wouldn't be sent on an errand somewhere where she couldn't watch for Nathan. She was also watching Running Deer so that she could stay away from the Indians. Pa would get her away from here. She wondered where Pa was. He was watching her, she knew. She stayed in the light of the fire so he could see her.

Where was Nathan? She knew that it was much longer than an hour since they had last met. Surely she couldn't have missed seeing him. What if he had already gone? What should she do? She couldn't bear to be in this village without him. Fear closed her throat at the thought of being left behind. "Stop it,

Sarah!" she shook herself. "You know Pa wouldn't leave you. You're gettin' fretted. Something has held Nathan back a while. He'll make sure you see him. He wouldn't leave you any more than Pa would," she told herself. "Get busy and keep watchin'."

She started gathering up scraps of meat and bones to feed to the dogs that, for once, were tied. Usually, they were underfoot everywhere in the village, but tonight they were kept out of the way—another thing to be thankful for, she realized.

As she walked back toward the women, she saw Nathan. Their eyes met, and Sarah knew that soon she would start counting to a hundred. Her heart was beating so hard she was sure it could be heard.

Sarah watched Nathan work his way slowly through the Indians. How could he be so calm? It seemed ages until he reached the woods. She started, "One, two, three...." She made herself take a breath between each number.

One-hundred! Time to go. She left the spit she had been tending and picked up the pails that were used to carry water. "Not so fast, Sarah, just act like you're going for water. Don't look around. Act natural, like Pa said." So she talked to herself all the way to the river. Never had it seemed so far away from the village. It was so hard not to run. Finally, she reached the dugout. "Nathan," she whispered as she crawled into it. A big hand closed over her mouth.

CHAPTER SEVENTEEN

A WALK IN THE WOODS

"Shh! Shhh! Sarah, it's me, Pa. Nathan's safe with Sam'l. I'll tell you later. As quiet as you can, go to that bush where I first talked to you and wait for me," he breathed into her ear. He lifted her over the side of the dugout and pointed her in the right direction.

Luke stepped out of the canoe and, leaving Sarah's and Nathan's footprints in the damp soil at the river's edge, he began to clear away all traces of his being anywhere near the canoe. He had already put several heavy stones into it. Slowly, he pushed it into the water and set it adrift. The current would take it downstream. He hoped to throw the Indians off the trail. Carefully backing toward the bush, he erased the tracks he and Sarah had made.

Now he took her hand and led her toward the water. He was careful to leave no trail. Together they stepped into the river, and Luke took Sarah on his back. Then he waded out until he was waist deep. Carrying Sarah, he began walking upstream, against the pull of the current, as quickly as he could. He walked for a good way before he came closer to the shore, where the going was easier. Finally, he headed to the shore. The forest at that place was thick and would give good cover.

He set Sarah on her feet and started into the trees. The pace he set was fast, and Sarah found it hard to keep up, but it wasn't fast enough for her. She was fearful of a recapture. Pa stopped and let her catch her breath for a moment. Then they started off again, moving uphill. It was harder going than ever.

Just as Sarah was feeling as though she couldn't get another full breath, Pa stopped again. He signaled that she should lie down on the ground, and he put his hand over her mouth to tell her not to speak. "I'll be back," he whispered. "Don't move."

At last, she had rested enough to raise her head. There was a glow that looked as though it were below the place where she lay. She crawled closer and saw that she was lying on a ridge far over the Indian village.

"Why had they come here? Where was Pa?"

From behind, a faint smell of bear grease and smoke came to her. She was afraid to turn her head.

CHAPTER EIGHTEEN

RUN FROM THE RIDGE

Without making a sound, Nathan crawled up next to Sarah. Slowly, she let out the breath she was holding. Of course he smelled of cooked meat and bear fat; she probably did, too—they'd been working around the cooking fire all day. She sure was skittish!

Pa came up on the other side of her. There was a big man with him. That must be Sam'l. Not one word was spoken as they watched the village.

The Indians were still dancing around the fire. Sarah realized that they had not yet been missed. By the looks of the woodpile by the cooking fire, she figured they'd been gone about an hour. The heap of logs had gone way down. She was supposed to keep the pile up. Little Bird would soon wonder why Sarah hadn't carried more wood and would start looking for her.

Just as she had predicted, Sarah soon saw that the women were going in and out of the quonsets. Next, they started looking in the dark places. The dance suddenly stopped, and the high voices of the Indians faintly rose from the clearing. They knew the children were gone. The braves began to search along the edge of the woods. Several of them went into the forest. They had found Nathan's trail. Another party headed for the river. It took them only seconds to discover that the dugout had been pushed into the water and to find the tracks of Sarah and Nathan leading to it.

The alarm was sounded. The group of braves that had tracked Nathan burst out of the woods near the river. The Indians wasted no time. It was all too clear to them that the children had stolen a canoe and escaped. Quickly, they pushed the other canoes into the water and began to paddle downstream. That was what Luke had been waiting to see. The Indians had taken the bait. Now was the time to move—before they discovered that they had been tricked. When they did find out, they'd be as mad as hornets, Luke thought. They were mad enough now losing their captives, and their being children would make the Indians even madder. We'd better get away fast and make sure we don't get caught. If they catch us, they'll show no mercy.

He reached over Sarah and touched Nathan's shoulder as a signal to move. Taking Sarah's hand again, he pulled her to her feet. He squeezed her hand once, though, to say everything would be all right. As quietly as they could move, they started off into the woods. They had to make as much distance as they could. The Indians couldn't read tracks in the dark.

Luke led the way, pulling Sarah behind him. Nathan followed, and Sam'l brought up the rear. They kept moving, except for a few short rest stops, until daybreak. Sarah was more tired than she had ever been. She felt like she'd been walking in her sleep half the time. At last they stopped in a sheltered place. It was where the water had washed out part of a hill and the dirt made a kind of overhang. Gratefully, Sarah sank to the ground. Nathan lay down beside her. For the second time since they'd been taken, he slept with his arm over her.

Sam'l backtracked a ways and made sure they hadn't left a trail. Luke sat guard over his son and daughter and hoped to get them back safely to the fort. He brushed a tear from his eye and muttered, "I'm tryin', Lizabeth, I'm tryin'."

Once in the fort, he would tell where the other captives were. It would be their responsibility to get the other captives back from the Indians. He wished he could have freed them, too. He would be lucky to get these two to safety. Bad as it was, the others would have to wait.

Luke and Sam'l took turns, one on guard while the other slept. The children had been asleep about four hours when they were awakened. They didn't take time to eat. They started chewing on strips of jerky as they kept up a steady pace. They would travel until Sarah could go no farther without rest.

They were making good time until Sarah stumbled over a root and fell. She was so tired that she hadn't seen it. She tried to get up, but the pain in her ankle set her back down.

"Pa, I can't walk!" she cried, tears leaving little paths behind as they rolled down her dirty cheeks.

Luke knelt and felt of the bones. "It ain't broke. Just a bad pull, but you won't get nowhere on that foot." He looked around and saw some plantain leaves, which he picked. He wrapped them around Sarah's ankle, which was beginning to swell.

"I'll have to carry you. We can't stop here. It's too open."

"Luke, there's a cave of sorts somewhere close to here. I hunted this way a couple of years ago. If I remember right, it should be over this way," Sam'l said. He started off to the left. The others followed. It didn't take him long to find the cave. Luke laid Sarah on the floor inside, where she quickly went to sleep again.

"Looks safe enough, Sam'l. Don't know as I could have carried her far. She's an armload, though she don't look it. We've been pushin' hard. Guess we all could use a rest. I'm goin' to fashion a litter to carry Sarah. We can make better time than wearin' ourselves down carryin' her in turns."

"I'll help you, Luke. Ain't no Indians close to us yet."

They went into the forest to cut two saplings to use for poles and to find wild grape vines with which to lace them together. It would make a bed of sorts, on which Sarah could lie to be carried. They would be gone just a few minutes. The children were both asleep and safe enough, they thought.

Shortly after they left, an Indian stepped from behind a tree and cautiously started toward the cave. He appeared to be alone. He stepped into the mouth of the cave.

Sarah had tossed and turned, troubled by her dreams. The pain in her sprained ankle woke her, and she opened her eyes.

"Running Deer!"

With one long step, he reached Sarah. He scooped her up into his arms and headed for the trees. She was so terrified she couldn't even scream.

CHAPTER NINETEEN

TRY AGAIN

"Stop! Put that girl down!" Luke and Sam'l stepped out from the trees in front of the Indian. Both of them were pointing their rifles at the Indian.

"How in tarnation did you think you'd steal her again?" Luke asked.

The Indian stood silent before them, his head bowed. How could the white man know how he felt? He had lost much respect when the girl escaped. He loved her and had planned to name her as his bride at the ceremony and take her into the lodge of his father. She was his prize. She should have been proud to be chosen by Running Deer, brave warrior of the Shawnee. He had watched her all through the feasting. She had worked well. He felt that she would make a good wife for him after she learned the ways of the women.

When she had disappeared, he continued searching for signs of her even after dark. He must get her back. He had shown her that he had singled her out. Now she had scorned him and shamed him by running away.

It didn't seem to matter what happened to him now. He was disgraced. He could not go back to the tribe.

"What'll we do with this varmint, Luke?"

Luke studied the problem for a few minutes. He made up his mind. "We'll take him with us to the fort, Sam'l. We can use him to get the other captives back. The Indians will be movin' now that the hunt is over. Probably head back across the river where they belong. He'll know where the village moved."

Sam'l kept his rifle pointed at Running Deer while Luke went for Nathan and the litter they had made to carry Sarah.

They lifted Sarah onto it. Luke picked up the front poles and motioned for Running Deer to take the back. Sam'l, never taking his gun off Running Deer's back, followed them. Nathan took the lead.

Nathan had learned much about tracking from the Indians while on the hunting parties. Luke had to direct him only a few times.

Before they had started, Sam'l had gone back over the Indian's route and made sure that he was alone. He wondered how Running Deer had known that Sarah and Nathan were not in the canoe that had been sent adrift downstream. They questioned him, but he remained mute. Sam'l and Luke knew there was no way to make an Indian talk if he didn't want to. They'd probably never find out.

As they hiked through the forest, Running Deer kept alert for a chance to escape. He knew that Sam'l would shoot him, but if he could get away, he would bide his time until the settlers thought they were safe. Then he would kidnap the girl again and return in glory to his people.

Right now, it looked like he'd have to be patient and do what these men wanted.

Running Deer knew how to be patient. It was a lesson he'd been taught early. For days, he had watched at the cabin until he saw that it was a good time to signal his men to raid. He'd waited at the camp seeing Sarah work with the women until he knew that she would be a good wife for him. Then he had decided to choose her. When the braves had followed the dugout and found it empty against the bank of the river, he had not given up. Carefully, he'd gone over the ground on both sides of the village until he'd found the place where Luke and Sarah had come out of the water. Then he followed their trail, backtracking when he'd lost it. He'd not slept nor eaten but pushed on until he had been captured. Now the Indian knew that the lessons of patience had been forgotten in his eagerness to save his honor. Running Deer shrugged. It was time to wait and watch again.

As they made their way through the forest, Sarah watched Running Deer. "What was there about him that frightens me so?" she wondered. She had no fear now, because Pa and Sam'l were there. Rubbing the scar on her wrist, she looked at him, curiously. He looked like any other Indian as far as she could tell. She was glad that he was carrying the foot of the litter. He smelled like any other Indian, too. However, there was something about him that bothered her. What could it be? His hair was black and tied in the Shawnee way. Dark eyes glittered from the copper color of his face. His body was lean and glistened with grease.

He shifted his hands to get a better grip on the poles he carried. Sarah was drawn to the movement to look at them. Her eyes widened in surprise as she saw his wrist. There were thong marks on it, too, just like hers. He, too, had once been a captive. But by whom?

CHAPTER TWENTY

THE INDIAN WAY

When they arrived at the clearing in front of the fort, a big cheer went up. They must look like a bedraggled band coming out of the woods, thought Sarah. Several men ran out to help. Two took the litter and carried Sarah the rest of the way to Martha's house. Some others bound Running Deer's hands and put a noose over his head, tightening it around his chest and dragging him into the fort. The women prepared a feast that evening, as everyone was relieved that Luke and Sam'l had rescued Sarah and Nathan.

After they had been at the fort for several weeks, Sarah's ankle finally healed and returned to normal. Pa had told the men about the captives and the Indian villages, and some of the men had gone to see if they could recover some or all of the other captives.

Since they had reached the fort, Running Deer had been locked in a cabin that was used for storage. There was no window in it. Someone always stood guard at the door. He had been questioned for days, but they got nothing from him. He lay on his pallet and refused to eat. He had lived as an Indian too long to even remember a time when he was taken. Being watched so closely showed him that there was no way he could escape.

Sarah often thought about him while her ankle was mending. When she was able to walk, she made up her mind to find out more about him. She no longer feared him; instead, she felt a curious sympathy for him. Both of them had been captured. If Pa hadn't saved her in time, she, too, might have become as much an Indian as Running Deer.

She had gone to the cabin where he was kept. She went to the door and called to him through the small opening that let air into the little room where he lay.

He took no more notice of her than he did of anyone else. "Running Deer," she called. "I want to talk to you. Come to the door."

"Running Deer," she tried again. "It's Sarah. I want to help you. Tell me who your parents are. I know you were captured. If we can find your folks, you can go back to them."

He lay as though he had turned to stone.

Slowly, Sarah turned away. She tried twice more, without any success, to get him to respond.

Luke tried to explain to her that the young man had lived with the Indians for so long that he believed himself to be one. This often happened when a boy is captured so young. It could have happened to Nathan.

Trapped in a shed, Running Deer turned his face to the wall. What did the girl know about freedom? He saw no way out of his shame. He would not live as a caged animal. He made up his mind he would escape or die. It was the Indian way.

CHAPTER TWENTY-ONE

DECISION

"Pa, when are we goin' home?" Nathan asked. "It's high time we got the corn in the ground. I was talkin' to Matthew the other day, and he said he had some extra corn seed he could let us have."

Luke had been thinking, too. The confinement of the fort was beginning to wear on him. There were too many people around. Particularly widow Schmidt, a former teacher, and her endless chatter. She gave him the willies. He also knew that her first name was Jane and she was a beautiful and lonely lady. She had light red hair and blue eyes. She had told him that she had come from Ireland but had married an elderly German man, who had died over a year ago. Sometimes he wished that he had the patience to know her better, as he knew that he didn't want to live alone for the rest of his life. But he had been so hurt by Lizabeth's death that he was afraid to risk loving another woman again. He was used to the quiet of the woods and longed to return.

Living in the cabin with James and his family troubled Luke. They were already crowded before they added three more people. Martha, James's wife, was a good woman. She was always bustling about, helping everyone, but her tongue was never still. Her constant chatter often drove Luke out of the house.

Lizabeth had been easy about her work. She never seemed to be in a hurry. Everything she had to do was done when it should be, but without the flutter that Martha had about her. His wife had never felt the need to talk about every little thing that went on. When she had something to say she said it, and that was only after she thought it out before she spoke.

Sarah was enamored with Martha. Martha helped Sarah with her reading and learning to speak the English language like a lady. Luke could understand the attraction, as Martha was the first woman Sarah could talk to since their capture.

Gramma's death and the death of Ben and Mary were hard for Sarah and Nathan. Luke didn't think Sarah would stop crying after he told her. He had saved that bad news until they got to the fort. Nathan was stoic. He had suspected as much anyway.

Luke missed Gramma and the small children. He didn't want to go home and see their graves, nor did he want to stay in the fort. The conflict was deep inside him. On the one hand, he would like to give up and go back to Pennsylvania. On the other, he had promised the children that they could rebuild the cabin and have a fresh start. For the first time in his life, he didn't know what to do.

Sarah decided for him. She knew it was time to go.

"Let's go home, Pa. There ain't nothin' in the fort for us. Ain't much left back home either, but you promised Ma when you built the stone chimney it would last a lifetime. Lets go see if you were right."

BOOK TWO

REEDS IN THE WILDERNESS

CHAPTER ONE

IT'S GOOD TO BE HOME

"Pa! Pa! I can still see the chimney! It's still there! You really did build it to last a lifetime!"

It had been a year since they had last seen their home. Sarah pushed aside a bush at the edge of the overgrown clearing and stepped from the lush forest into the sunlight.

"Looks like the trees have started growing up from the stumps already. Didn't seem like we'd been gone that long, Pa. Things sure do sprout fast in a Kentucky springtime."

Nathan looked around and shook his head at the weed-covered field that had to be cleared out before the corn could be planted. He looked at the remains of the cabin and again shook his head.

"It's going to take a lot of work to put this place back together," he remarked.

Luke looked over at the grass-covered graves at the side of the clearing. Luke seemed older than a man in his late 30s. He was already showing some gray hair, and a few of his whiskers in his beard also had some gray. His deep blue eyes were sad and seemed sunken back into his head. As the father of the family, Luke had experienced the death of his wife, Lizabeth, and baby daughter Beth. Then an Indian raid had cost Gramma and two other children, Ben and Mary, their lives. The Indians had burned the cabin and kidnapped both Sarah and Nathan. Luke felt responsible for his family and considered it a tragic defeat that the Indians had captured two of his children and had killed the two younger ones and Gramma. Luke walked over to the graves and said, "Lizabeth, I brought the family back. I promised you that I would. I am so sorry about Gramma and the young'uns. I'm a-goin' to rebuild this cabin, and we *will* be family again."

Sarah and Nathan stayed respectfully back as their father stood at the gravesite. Both of them recalled their being taken captive by the Indians. Luke and a friend, Sam'l, had rescued them from the Indians and had taken them to the Fort. They knew that their father would have searched for them until he found them or had died in the effort. Sarah and Nathan had an enormous respect for their father. When he said he would do something, they knew he would do it.

Now they were back at the homestead. It wasn't the same without Gramma. It wasn't the same as before the cabin was burned down and had sat over the past winter as a burned out shell. But the stone chimney stood like a monument to the family. It was the centerpiece of the great room of the cabin, and it had been built to last a lifetime.

Several years before, Luke and Lizabeth decided to sell out in Pennsylvania and move to Kentucky, which was not a state at that time. It was a County of Virginia, where the land was free for the taking and working of it. They carried everything they could from Pennsylvania to their new home. Sarah and Nathan were young but they had to carry their share. Gramma, in spite of her age, had to carry a large load of material.

The family had a good beginning. They had planted corn and vegetables the first year and had enough to last them through the first winter. Firewood was plentiful, so they never froze in their cabin, like many settlers did. Luke and Lizabeth worked very hard the second summer and put a wooden floor in the cabin and a loft in the upper part. It was that summer that Luke, with help from everyone else, had built the magnificent stone chimney. Now it was the only thing left standing in the ashes of what remained of their home.

Sarah, Nathan and Luke stood at the edge of the woods and looked at the ruin that lay before them. Luke slumped down and said, "Children, I don't think I can rebuild this place. I just don't have it in me anymore."

Sarah was the first to speak up. "Pa, we can do it. You can do it. Nathan and I will help. Please, Pa, let's do it. Let's rebuild the cabin."

Nathan was more of a realist. "Pa, it will be a lot of work, but we can. We must! This is our home. Ma, Gramma and the young'uns are buried here. This is our land!"

Tears rolled down Luke's cheeks as he drew both children to him. He just nodded his head. They all understood.

Sarah broke the silence. "I remember long days bent over that iron kettle over there and stirring food for the family. I remember sitting on that stoop and watching fireflies flash on and off until I was so sleepy that someone had to carry me to bed."

"I remember how good the stews smelled waiting to be eaten," Nathan remarked.

"Somehow, Ma and Gramma would take the toughest old rabbit or squirrel and make a feast out of it." Nathan's shoulders slumped as he remembered his mother and Gramma.

Often, Gramma would call Nathan to the door and hand him a juicy, hot fried pie that she had made. Gramma seemed partial to Nathan, and no matter how much Nathan had eaten he always had room for something sweet. Nathan had grown a lot in the past year. He was now fourteen and had broadened out in the shoulders. He was taller than Sarah by a little bit and was becoming very strong. "Hard work will build muscles," Gramma used to say.

Nathan's dark blond hair was long, and he had it tied behind his neck with a piece of leather thong. He had his father's deep blue eyes, but he was built sturdier than Luke. He was built more like Gramma. On the frontier, fourteen was considered a man, and Nathan could do a man's work.

Luke brushed tears from his eyes and tried to blot out the images of the bodies of Gramma, Ben and Mary that he had found when he returned from the hunt. In his memory, he could still see the smoke rising from the ashes and smell the acrid odors mixed with that smoke and the dried blood of those he had to bury. "Maybe we should give up and go back east," he remarked.

"No, Pa, no, this is our home." Sarah said quietly.

Luke was aware of how important rebuilding was to Sarah and Nathan. They had not seen the carnage at the cabin, and their only memory was the capture. They now were faced with the graves for the first time. The five graves were as heartbreaking as Luke could stand. Sarah knew of her father's grief but was determined to keep the family in tact and here in Kentucky.

As Luke struggled to control his emotions he vowed to give the children the home that they had lost, even though he would have to fight the demons in his own mind. He knew that hard work would help him sleep better at night. He walked away from the children, kicking bits of charred wood as he walked. Finally, he squared his shoulders, cleared his throat and said, "Wonder if there's anything else left that didn't burn up? Guess we'll have to sift through these ashes to see if there's anything we can use. I doubt that we'll find much. Looks like the fire was pretty hot."

"The ashes will be awful dirty, too, Pa," Sarah said. "We sure will be filthy by the time we get through with this mess. I don't mind being grubby, but I like to be able to get clean when I'm done working."

Sarah, a little over fifteen, was becoming a real beauty. Her blond hair accented her tanned skin. Her deep blue eyes and perfect teeth made her broad smile a cherished possession and assured her popularity at the Fort. She was tall, thin and almost a woman, with attributes of kindness and helpfulness. Many of the young men at the Fort dreamed about Sarah as their bride. Sarah was not yet ready for a suitor, however. She had been badly frightened in the Indian village when the Indian, Running Deer, wanted her for himself as his bride. Sarah was scared by that experience.

"You sound just like your Ma, Sarah," observed her father. "She liked to keep things clean, too. Well, we can't just stand here all day looking. Let's get busy and try to see what we can find. We'll put these packs we're carrying over there under those two little trees near the cabin," Luke said as he walked toward the burned-out ruin, "then we'll start searching from there."

They stacked the skin-covered backpacks in the shade to protect their contents, the supplies and food they needed to get started again. Everything they brought with them had been a gift from the people in the Fort. Sarah carried all the seeds for planting. They brought enough meat to last them until they could hunt. Nathan and Luke carried tools and materials for rebuilding. Each had a bed roll, which was tied across the top of the pack. Between them, Nathan and Luke had carried a plow head that had belonged to Sam'l.

People living on the frontier would share whatever was available, knowing that a tragedy could befall them at any time. When another person needed something, it was the code of the hills to share. No one would think of not sharing.

93

Close to the trees was the ash-hopper, standing crookedly but partly filled with ashes that Gramma had put into it to make lye for the soap. She had just started that chore when the cabin was raided.

Sarah stood the hopper straight and walked toward the chimney, stirring up dust from the charred wood. She stubbed her toe on something hard, only to find that it was the large rock they called "the stoop." It sat right outside the door of the cabin so that when it rained they didn't step from the mud onto the clean plank floor. As she brushed the ashes from it, she remembered how Pa and Nathan had built a rough log sled and then had struggled with the stone until they finally got it up by the door. There it lay as a permanent fixture for the foundation of the cabin. Ma had been well pleased to have the big stone there because it served as a stepping-stone into the cabin and a big front stoop, just like back in Pennsylvania. Ma had planted some seeds by the stoop—seeds that grew into gourds. The flowers had looked very pretty against the log walls of the cabin, and later the gourds could be dried and used to make drinking utensils and other things.

Sarah sat for a moment with her back to the burned cabin, tears in her eyes, and tried to pretend that things were as they used to be. Then her attention was drawn to something big and black off to the side of the cabin.

Curious, she walked over to see what it was. "Pa! Come what I've found! It's the big iron kettle! Gramma had it outside to make soap. Help me move it over to the hopper. I'm going to make a little soap right now. We can be clean even though we're living as rough as can be."

"Sarah, what will you use for fat? You got to have fat to make soap."

"I can trim some of the fat off the meat we brought. It will only make a little soap, though. Later on, when you and Nathan go hunting, I'll make some more. Just don't bring me any bear fat. I smelled enough bear grease in the Indian village to last me a lifetime. I don't think I ever want to smell bear grease again. I know I would get sick."

While Pa set the kettle where she wanted it, Sarah went toward the creek to strip bark from a birch tree. She had learned in the Indian village how to make birch bark buckets for carrying water. She had learned many uses for birch bark from the Shawnees who had held her captive. They had even used strips of the white bark to cover their wigwams. Pa had said that you can get something good out of anything, no matter how bad it seems when the times may seem very bad.

After Sarah finished making the bucket, she went to the hearth of the chimney and scraped some ashes from the back of it into her bucket. She carried them to the hopper and added them to those that Gramma had put in. Then she went to the stream for water. As she poured the water over the ashes, she said to herself, "With the ashes that Gramma'd put in, and these new ashes, I should be able to make good soap. Maybe Gramma's skill will drain through and help me."

It would be a while before the water seeped through and made lye from the ashes. Then it was necessary to drain the lye into the kettle. The girl went back to the packs, unwrapped the meat, and began carefully to trim the fat from the meat. There wasn't as much as she would have liked, but some fat was better than no fat at all. She piled it on a rock and waited for the lye to become ready. "I don't have anything to stir with. The soap won't be any good unless it's stirred often. Guess I'll have to make a paddle," she said aloud to herself.

Sarah looked around until she found a straight, thick branch of pine. Then she took a hatchet from the pack and hacked away at the log until the bark was off. She chipped at the wood on the end until she had flattened it enough to stir the mixture. The pine would make the soap smell good, as well.

Sarah walked down to where Pa and Nathan were working and saw a stack of poles. They were stripping bark from several trees farther into the woods.

"What are you doing? We've got so much cleaning up to do, and you're cutting wood."

"We have to build a lean-to, Sarah. We need someplace to put things in case it rains. It won't be much, but it'll keep us dry. We won't be able to stand up and walk around in it." Pa explained. "Nathan, I think that's enough bark. We can set these poles and maybe finish up before dark."

Sarah started back to build a fire under the kettle. Luke and Nathan set the fork-topped poles into the ground at an angle. Then they set another forked pole into the ground, standing straight up from the ground under each pole's fork. These poles held up the ends of the slanted poles. Pa notched the straight poles and, starting from the ground up, laid them across the frame so that the notches fit the poles. When he finally reached the top of the framework he had a sturdy lean-to ready for the birch bark. Nathan carried the strips of bark to Luke, who bent the tip and, again starting at the ground, laid the birch bark like shingles. The second row covered part of the first row, making it almost watertight. It was slow work because Luke believed that any job worth doing should be done as well as possible. It was almost dusk when they finished. The last thing Luke did was to lay more poles over the shingles to hold them down until they dried out. The weight of the poles would also help to prevent shingles from blowing off in case a wind blew up. The front of the lean-to was open. Finally, they stood back and looked at it.

"That's a fair job, I guess," Pa said to Nathan. "Anyway, it'll do for keeping things out of the weather until we can build something better."

Nathan said, "It'll do, Pa. I wonder if Sarah has her soap done?"

"That girl sure likes to be clean. Let's go and see if we are going to have supper," Luke said.

"Maybe it's soap we're eating," Nathan groaned when he saw Sarah bent over the kettle, stirring.

"Nathan, you know Mama and Gramma taught me better than that. I've got strips of meat roasting on sticks at the side of the fire. I found some potatoes in that special bundle that Martha stuck in my pack. They're in the coals cooking, too. You'd better eat them slow because I'm fixing to plant the rest in my garden patch. There's something else in there to plant, but it's going to surprise you. I just hope it won't short Martha in her planting. I believe she'd beggar herself to share with us."

"Yes, Martha's a good woman," Pa admitted. "She took us in when we had no place to go and treated us like family. It's too bad the fort is so far away, Sarah. It would be good for you to have her advice and help. I know it ain't going to be easy for you, taking on a woman's chores so young and not havin' another woman to talk to."

"Now, Pa, I'm more than half grown. There were girls in the Indian village no older than me who were married already."

"Yes, and you almost became an Indian bride," Nathan chimed in.

Pa looked at Nathan and said, "Those were Indian ways." Then to Sarah he said, "You're still my little girl. I wish you'd stayed at the fort until we had this place in better shape than it is now. You could have stayed with Martha. This living is too rough for a young girl."

"Pa, I ain't going to hear no more. When we first came here, we didn't have this much, and we made out. At least we have a chimney, and that's more than was here before."

"We also had Ma and Gramma," Nathan interjected.

Sarah sighed and said, "You go down to the creek and wash up. The meat is about done, and I need to stir my soap again. It's about done, too. Bring back a bucket of water for us to drink, and we'll be ready to eat."

Sarah smiled to herself as she overheard Nathan grumbling as they left for the creek.

The family sat around the fire after Luke had moved the kettle so the soap would cool. They were tired from the work and the long trek they had made that day, but it was a *good* tired feeling. They all had a positive feeling about making a home again. It felt right to be back at their homestead.

"I sure hope the soap is good," Sarah worried. She had helped Mama and Gramma, but she had never made soap before by herself.

"I just hope you didn't put too much lye into it," Nathan teased. "I ain't looking forward to peeling off my skin just to be clean enough to suit you, Sarah."

"As dirty as you get, nobody would know that you had skin."

"How you two have enough energy to bicker beats me. There's so much to do; it wearies me just thinking about it."

Nathan threw another log on the fire, and they sat around, just happy to be home.

After a period of silence, Luke said, "We need to think about how we're going about this. We can't go fifteen ways at once."

"Well, Pa," Nathan responded, "I guess we need to get the corn in. The signs are about right for planting and its getting late in the season to get it planted."

"You're right, Nathan. It will take us a couple of days to get the ground back in shape for planting. We'll have to plow under all those weeds in the fields. I'd hoped to break in a new field this year, but we'll have to wait on that. It takes too long to clear a field and plant it to do it this year."

"While you're plowing could you plow me up a garden place? I have things that need to go into the ground soon, too." Sarah interrupted.

"We'll try to, Sarah. If the weather holds, we can. Looks like we should have clear skies for a while. Once the seed's in, we'll want rain."

"Sarah, if we have to wait that long for rain, we ain't going to have corn growing, and that means slim eating over the winter."

"Oh, Pa, I know that! It just would be nice to have a proper roof leaning on that lonesome chimney sticking up in the sky all by itself."

"Well, the first thing we need to do is put the corn and garden in. Then we'll have to think about where to put the new cabin."

"Pa!" both Sarah and Nathan cried, "It will go back were it was. The chimney is already there."

"But the old cabin is full of ashes. It's almost impossible to get all the ashes out of where the cabin was. It's a big and dirty job."

"Pa, I'll scoop out the ashes and sift through them while you and Nathan get the corn in. Please, Pa, let's build the cabin where it was. It will be more like our home."

"I think so, too," Nathan said. "Pa, Sarah's right. We need to build it where it was. It will mean a lot more to me to have it there."

"Well, maybe. I suppose, after we get the corn and garden in, we could start cutting logs. It's late. We should go to sleep if we are to get up early tomorrow."

99

Sarah yawned. "Pa, I'm ready for sleep. It's been a long, long day. In the morning, we can use some of the soap I made and start the day clean."

"In the morning, Sarah, we can start plowing the field, then we'll worry about getting clean and using your soap." Nathan got his blanket, rolled up into it, and, with his feet to the fire, fell asleep.

"Goodnight, Pa, it's good to be home," Sarah said and almost instantly fell fast asleep.

Luke walked slowly over to the gravesite. He sat down and quietly said, "Lizabeth, I don't know if I can do it. I know what Sarah and Nathan want, but I don't know if I could or should try to rebuild here. There is much more work here than a man and two children can do, but the young'uns do want a home here. I don't know what to do."

CHAPTER TWO

TREASURES IN THE ASHES

"I'm sure glad that we brought Sam'l's hand plow along to use, Pa. Since we don't have a horse to pull a plow, it will be slow going with just one of us plowing."

"Yep, it's a good thing he could spare it. It plumb wears a body out to plow. At least, going over the old field ain't as bad as breaking new ground. Nathan, while I'm fitting handles to this plow of Sam'l's, you go and get started with ours. The Indians don't have a need for a plow or they would have taken ours, too. Maybe we'd be better if we planted with sticks, they way they do."

They were all anxious to get the field ready for the seed. In a couple of days, the moon would be growing. The settlers all knew that crops that grew above ground should be planted when the moon was in the early quarter. They had great faith in planting when the signs and times were right.

It was late for them to be planting, but with favorable weather they still could get a good crop. The seeds that Matthew had given them appeared to be well chosen. They were thankful that he was a careful farmer who kept more seed corn than he would need for his own crop.

Luke was trimming a piece of oak branch to make a handle for the plow. He had looked until he found a piece that had lain long enough to be seasoned. It was harder to trim, seasoned wood as it was, but it would be less likely to break than freshly cut wood.

Sarah poured the cooled soap into her birch bucket. She would have to make another bucket to carry water, but that would be easy. There was plenty of birch around.

She was anxious to get started sifting through the ashes of the cabin, but first she needed water. Quickly, she worked on another bucket. When Pa had time, he'd make her a bucket out of oak. It would hold more water than the bucket of birch. After cleaning out the big kettle, she put several small pieces of wood on the fire. The stew was started for their supper so that it would be ready when they finished their work. As she came from getting water, Sarah picked several wild onions that were growing in the field. They would give the stew a good flavor. If she could find some peppergrass that had gone to seed, she would use the seed to flavor the meat.

The stew was cooking and the blankets were rolled and stored in the lean-to. She decided to start on the cabin. There was a flat piece of bark that could be used to lift the ashes and scrape through them after the chunks of charred wood were pulled out.

"Guess the best place to start is at the chimney and work my way to the other end of the cabin. No sense going at this willy-nilly," Sarah said to herself. "Think I'll mark off a place on the side and look through it, then go on to the next part. That way, I know that I won't miss anything. Whew! This burned out wood is sure dirty, smelly stuff."

For over an hour, she pulled pieces of logs from the ashes and carried them down to where they had a fire in front of the lean-to. Soon there was a pile of black, shiny, half burned logs. Sarah's face and hands were a black as the pile of logs. She was glad that she had put on the clothes of skins that she had worn in the Indian village. Skins were hot, but if she'd had on her dress, it would have been ruined.

Sifting through the ashes stirred up much dust. Soon Sarah's eyes were burning, and she could hardly see. "There's got to be a better way to do this. I'm doing nothing but getting dirtier and dirtier. Maybe I can find a branch with lots of shoots that I can use for a rake. That would be better."

The raking went better than she thought. Over near the wall where the shelf had been lay a lump of dull metal. "What is this?" she wondered. "Pa will know." She laid it on the hearth. Soon there was a collection of things for Pa to see. There was the cast iron mold he used to make balls for his rifle. Next to it was the head of an axe. The handle had burned away. The blade of Ma's knife was so black that Sarah had almost missed seeing it. Pa could whittle new handles for these tools, and they'd be as good as new. She stood looking at the things she had found. Pa would be pleased, especially for his mold.

"The skillet! That's cast iron, too. It wouldn't burn. It should be here somewhere around the fireplace. I'll try the other side. I need that skillet." Dropping her branch, she felt around in the ashes with her hands. "Here it is! It was hiding in the corner under that big pile of ashes. Glory be! I'm happy to find you."

She hugged the skillet to her chest and did a little dance of joy. "Maybe I'd better do a little more thinking about what could be where. Might save myself some trouble. I'm going to wash this skillet and start using my head."

She carried the skillet down to the stream. The water looked so clean and fresh, and she was so hot and dirty. It didn't take her long to decide to be clean, too. Stripping off her clothes, she got into the water. She scrubbed herself as clean as she could with a handful of sand she'd scooped from the bottom. That made her feel much better. She dried herself with leaves and quickly put on her clothes. "What would Gramma say if she saw me washing myself in the creek with no clothes on? She'd really be put out with me. Well, at least my skin is clean, and Gramma would like that."

Sarah looked around the creek's bank. It sure was pretty down here. That big, old oak tree must have been there for a hundred years. She walked toward it. On the ground lay the pole with which Nathan had been fishing on the day he was captured. Sarah picked it up and saw that the hook was still on it. Maybe she'd try to catch a fish. Pa would like that for his supper. She found some grubs under a piece of rotted wood and went upstream to try her luck.

As she fished, she thought about what they would do when the meat ran out. Pa and Nathan could get plenty of rabbits and squirrels near the cabin until they had time to hunt for deer. She wished Pa would shoot a wild turkey. He wouldn't be likely to do that until the eggs were hatched and the chicks were able to take care of themselves. Pa was sure particular about things like that. He said no young should be left on their own until they'd learned to do for themselves.

The woods would furnish them with greens and roots to eat until the corn and garden were ready. Soon the wild strawberries would be ripe and they would feast on them, too. Later on, the blueberries, raspberries and blackberries would ripen. There were many wild grapevines close by. In the fall there would be nuts to gather. They'd not be hungry, at any rate.

"I ain't doing much good fishing. Guess I ain't got the right touch. I'd better get back before Pa thinks the Indians got me again." She put the pole back at the oak tree and, carrying the skillet, went up to the clearing.

"What have you been doing, Sarah? I saw you go to the creek a long time ago. I was just going to start looking for you."

"I'm sorry I fretted you, Pa. I was trying to catch a fish."

"Sarah, we ain't got time for fishing yet. We'll do that later when we can. Is there some water handy? Plowing makes for a dry throat."

"Here, Pa there's some in the bucket. Look what I found in the ashes, Ma's skillet. It didn't burn. I took it to the creek to wash it, and I found Nathan's fishing pole. I thought about using the skillet, and that's how I got started fishing. Guess I was thoughtless. I'm sorry, Pa."

"That's all right, Girl. Guess I'm still fearful for you since you was took by the Shawnees. It ain't safe even though the hunting parties have gone back to the villages now. When we get things in shape, we'll all go fishing. Now, show me what you found."

Sarah took him to the chimney. "Pa, what's this lump? It looks melted, and I don't know whether to keep it or not."

"Why, that's lead! It was on the shelf. It's soft, so it melts easy. I can use it to make shot. It can be melted over again and, since you found the mold, I can make balls for the rifle. I brought enough powder from the fort, but lead is hard to come by. This means I'll be able to get meat all winter." Pa patted Sarah's shoulder. He was pleased with the axe blade and knife. "Seems there was a froe inside, too, and an auger. That's the twisty-looking thing I used to make holes. You might look for a drawing knife, too. Remember the blade I used when I made the shingles for the roof of the cabin? This broadax is what I used to smooth the sides of the logs. We can get the cabin started sooner than I thought, since you found these tools. It won't be a big job to put handles on them."

"I'll find them, Pa. I remember now where they were. And maybe the flint we used to light the fire is in the ashes, too. That wouldn't burn."

"How about Pa's whetstone to sharpen the blades?" Nathan asked as he came up behind them.

"And the grinding stone for cornmeal? How could I forget that? I'd better get to raking again."

Nathan and Pa laughed at Sarah's rake. "Since you found so many things, Sarah, I'll make you a proper rake tonight when it's too dark to plow. Right now, I'd better get back or we won't have any corn to grind this year."

"Pa, I'll have your food ready when you get through. You and Nathan can take some of my soap and go to the creek and clean up before you eat. That water sure feels good, and it takes the kinks out."

Pa laughed. It wasn't the fishing that had taken Sarah so long. "Seems like you just ain't happy 'less you're clean, child," he laughed as he went back to the field.

In the evening, sitting around the fire, they were still busy. Pa was making a new rake for Sarah. He had whittled teeth for it. Now he was making holes in a larger log with the auger Sarah had found. Nathan was making a handle for the broadax, and Sarah was whittling on some small pieces of maple.

"What are you doing, Sarah?"

"I'm making spoons, Nathan. I ain't going to live like a heathen without proper dishes. I aim to have us something to eat with. Everyone dipping out of the same kettle is too messy for me."

"I guess we'll have to spruce up every night, too, before you'll let us eat."

"Now, Pa, there ain't no need to tease. The water's running free down at the stream. Ain't no need to be dirty unless you want to be. Nobody with dirty hands is eating what I cook, especially since we have to eat out of the same kettle right now."

"Think her name should be 'Scrub' instead of Sarah, Pa. She gets more like Mama and Gramma every day. Next thing, she'll make us wipe our feet before we walk to the fire circle."

"That's all right Nathan, women like things orderly. Think we can finish the field tomorrow?"

"We need to try. It ain't too bad breaking it up. It's a good thing you went over it before we were captured. All that's keeping us from planting is the grass that grew up this spring, and that ain't too bad."

"The moon will be right for planting day after tomorrow. It's starting to feel close. Should rain in a couple of days. We need to get the seed into the ground before it rains."

"Rain will set us back considerable."

"It ain't going to rain tomorrow. The ground ain't sweating when we plow." Pa finished the rake and handed it to Sarah. "There, now you should be able to find a needle in those ashes."

"Well, I'm not going to look for anything tonight. There's a lot to be done tomorrow. I'm going to get my blanket and go to sleep. You can talk all night if you want to." Sarah got up and brought her blanket from the lean-to.

"I'm tired, too, Pa. Think I'll go to sleep. It's a good thing it ain't any hotter. The mosquitoes would be feasting on us."

Luke sat staring into the fire for a while. A tear slipped down his cheek. He thought of his dead wife and dead children and was overcome with his loneliness. He wanted to go over to the gravesite but said to himself, "No. I can't think about what is past; I need to think about what I need to do tomorrow. We'll just take it one day at a time for now. If it don't rain tomorrow, we can get the seed in by early the next day. It ain't a big field, but it will serve our needs. We're making out all right. The children are anxious to get things back the way they were. We can replace things, but the people are gone forever." His big frame shook with silent, despairing sobs while he watched the dying embers turn to ash.

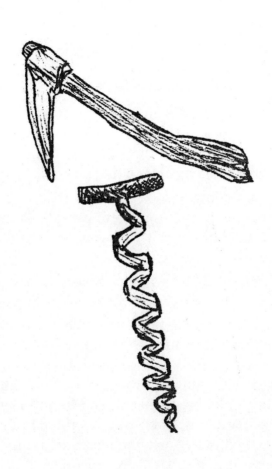

CHAPTER THREE

AN OLD FRIEND

L uke and Nathan were in the woods cutting trees for the cabin. The corn was planted and a gentle rain was falling. Sarah had found everything in the cabin remains that didn't burn in the fire. She felt she knew personally every ash there was in the ruins. She'd raked through all of it.

Luke had marked off the corners of the one-room cabin they planned to build, and Sarah was stacking stones for the corners where he had told her they must go. She had cleared out the fireplace and was cooking the squirrel that Nathan had shot that morning.

It began raining harder. Sarah stopped raking ashes. It was good to have rain on her garden, but raking ashes in the rain was very messy. Moreover, she didn't like being wet.

"I'll go into the woods. The trees will keep me dry for a while. I'll see if I can find something to cook with the meat." She picked up her birch bucket and Mama's knife with the new handle that Pa had fixed and headed for the woods. At the edge of the woods stood several honey locust trees. They were small and thorny, but their pods were filled with beans. Shelled and soaked overnight, they would be good to boil for the next day's meal. Carefully avoiding the thorns, Sarah soon filled her basket with the beans.

"I'm going to make a basket to carry things. This little old bucket won't hold enough. I'm wearing myself out going back and forth with it," she decided as she carried the bucket to the lean-to. She emptied the locust pods onto the ground under the shelter. "I'll shell these later, when I get back."

In the woods again, she found toothwort. She could use the leaves and roots of that plant. It would taste rather strong cooked alone, so she added violets to her pail, and some young plantain leaves. "I wish the ground nuts were ready, but it's too early for them. Gramma always said she'd as soon have them baked as sweet potatoes any day. I'd better get back to the clearing. Pa doesn't like me to be in the woods alone. And, being real honest, it bothers me somewhat still."

Back inside the lean-to, Sarah looked at the riches she had gathered. "Ain't no need for anybody to starve in the spring. Now, the winter was different thing, especially when the snow blows so hard you can't see the woodpile. I am not looking forward to winter coming soon."

She sat at the open side of the shelter, out of the rain, and began to shell the beans from the locust pods. "Hope I picked enough for us to eat. There ain't much left when the pods are off. My pail was overflowing, and now the beans just cover the bottom good. It's raining too hard to go back for more. Pa and Nathan will be soaked to the skin. Of course, the trees will shelter them some."

She could hear the sounds as the axes bit deep into the trees. Pa was as anxious as Sarah to get the cabin built. The lean-to wasn't large enough for them to move about or to sleep comfortably. Now, with the rain, it would be damp and cold as well. There was so much work to be done it was almost frightening. At least, the trees could be felled in the rain. That was something to be thankful for.

Sarah wished that her garden place could have been plowed before the rain. In the bundle that Martha had put in her pack was a handful of dried beans to plant. They wouldn't be eating many of them this year. Sarah planned to save the beans she grew this year for next year's seed.

There was horseradish still growing at the edge of the garden, and some rhubarb. When the rain let up she would get some stalks of rhubarb and cook them. She knew that the leaves would have to be thrown away, as the leaves contained poison. "Wish I had some sweetening for the rhubarb. Maybe, if the rain eases, I can find some cane to cook with. That would help a little."

Luke and Nathan came to the lean-to. "We need to fix Nathan's axe. The handle broke when he was cutting down the last poplar tree we were cutting. Move over, Sarah, I'm wet as a beaver building a dam. No need for you to get wet from me."

"Pa, I was thinking about the cabin. When you build it, we'll need a loft. I aim to pick and dry enough berries and other food so we won't be hungry this winter. We thought we had plenty last fall when we were here, but the snow was so bad that we had to piece things out, and even then we almost ran out."

"There aren't as many of us now, Sarah." Luke reminded her.

"I know, but you never can tell what the weather will be. I never want to be hungry again if I can help it."

"Sarah, where did you put the whetstone? I'm going to sharpen these axe blades while Pa's making a new handle."

"Sharpen the broadax, too, Nathan. If we drag one of the logs down and the rain lets up, we can start squaring them off tonight."

"Pa, why don't you just leave the logs round like you did before?

111

"The water runs off them better when they're flat, and they last longer. I just peeled off the bark so's the bugs wouldn't have a nesting place under it. I'd have flattened the logs then, but I was in a hurry to build." Luke's voice trailed off into a whisper as he remembered the first cabin he built. He bit his lower lip in sorrowful anger.

"It will be good to have a roof over our heads again. I can't wait to sit on a real bench again 'stead of on grass, a rock or a log. How long do you think it will take?"

"Depends on the weather. Cutting the trees is the easy part. Making shingles for the roof takes time. We're going to need to make some locust wedges to use for making the shingles, Nathan. We'll use the wedge to split the trunks of the trees. With both of us working steady, we should be able to get enough in four or five days to cover the roof. I want to have everything ready for when Sam'l comes to help put up the cabin. He said he'd be out here in three or four weeks. I don't want to put him out of his time no more than I have to. He's got his own place to tend to."

"Pa, that handle looks good enough now. Let's go back and finish cutting that tree. Looks like the rain's letting up a bit."

When Luke and Nathan had gone, Sarah began tidying up the lean-to. "I need a broom. Pa sure left a mess with his wood shavings. Wish I had some broom straw, but I ain't. I'll have to get some from the rushes from down at the creek. They won't last as long but they'll do for now."

The rain had almost stopped when Sarah went to the creek to gather rushes. She also found cress growing there. That would be good to add to her greens. She cut a length of wild grapevine to bind the rushes to a stick that would become a broom handle. "Guess I look like a peddler," she laughed as she went back up the hill carrying the things she had found.

It took her only a few minutes to tie the rushes to the heavy stick. It felt good to be able to sweep again, even though the small floor of the lean-to was just dirt. If everything went well, soon she'd be sweeping a real floor.

The sleeping blankets were damp. They needed to be aired. Gramma aired the quilts almost every day. She said that airing them kept out the dust and they'd sleep better.

Sarah carried the blankets up to the bushes that Gramma had used to hang clothes on to dry and to air. She gave the bushes a good shake to knock off the raindrops that were still clinging. The sun had come out and it wouldn't be long until it dried the dampness of the blankets. She shook them out and draped them over the bushes while walking around to spread them evenly. At the back of the bush she stepped on something thick and soggy. It didn't feel like leaves. Looking down, she saw that there was a mass of wet, muddy cloth. She pulled at it until it was free from the overhang of the bush. It was so dirty that it was hard to tell want it was. As it was straightened out, she felt ridges through the mud that covered it. Then Sarah knew that it was the quilt that Gramma had treasured so much. She must have had it airing when the Indians attacked.

Gramma had really set store by that quilt. She'd always said that it was the story of her life. Often as they sat by the fire at night, Gramma got the quilt and told stories about pieces of cloth that had been put in the quilt. Sarah had sat on the floor and run her fingers over the fancy stitching that held the pieces together. Gramma had called it a crazy quilt because it had no pattern. It was made of large and small pieces of cloth that were still usable long after the dress or shirt from which they were cut had worn out.

Gramma had carried it over the mountains from Pennsylvania. She said it was the only thing she wouldn't leave or sell from the old place.

Sarah picked it up. It was like having Gramma back, in a way. A sharp pain went through Sarah and she said, "I sure miss you, Gramma." She walked to the creek to wash the quilt.

113

"I sure hope this quilt will hold together after laying in the weather for such a long time."

She swirled the quilt through the water to rinse off the mud. Then, laying it on a rock, she scrubbed it gently with some of the soap she had made. Without soap she would never have gotten the quilt clean. When it was rinsed in the clear running water, she could see the places where the cloth had rotted through. There wasn't anything she could do now. She would have to wait until she got some cloth from somewhere. She didn't know how long that would be, but it didn't really matter. She'd never part with it. Gramma said the quilt was a history of her lifetime. Sarah would add her own story to the places that were missing.

For the first time in a long time, Sarah sat down in the lean-to and sobbed. She realized she was alone in the wilderness with her father and her brother. The nearest woman was Martha, who was back at the fort. She knew how Pa felt and why he would rather give up than rebuild. She needed to pull herself together and not let Pa know how lonesome she was or how much she missed Gramma. She suddenly felt like the little girl that she was.

CHAPTER FOUR

CABIN RAISING

"Halloo! Luke! See you're ready for me." Sam'l came out of the woods toward the cabin where Luke and Nathan were stacking shingles for the roof.

Sam'l's rangy body was clothed in deerskins that seemed to blend into the woods. Nathan and Luke hadn't seen him until he was in the clearing. Even his sandy hair and beard were an extension of his clothes. His skin was weathered to match the rest of him, the woodsman that he was. He made no sound as he moved. The only thing about him that didn't blend in was the color of his eyes. They were blue, the blue of the waters of a deep, hidden lake. His eyes were constantly watching for game, or danger, or hazards.

"Yep! Sam'l, glad to see you. We've got the logs all squared up and the pieces cut for the rafters and the floor plate. The logs for the floor are cut, but we ain't pulled then down yet. We'll have to split 'em into boards. Nathan and I can do that later. We've been working on cutting the shingles. Putting 'em on is a three-man job. I don't aim to take any more of your time that I need to. It's mighty neighborly of you to come over to get the cabin raised."

"That's what friends are around for. You'd do the same for me. That meat sure smells good, Sarah. Looks like you're as good a hand at cooking as your Ma and Gramma were."

A squeaking noise came from the front of Sam'l's shirt. "Here, almost forgot about him." Sam'l pulled a bundle of brown fur from inside his shirt. "Guess I got so used to wearing him next to my skin I thought he was part of me. He's one of the litter from Squire's dog. He ain't big as a minute yet, but he should be a good watch dog in a few months."

Nathan took the puppy from Sam'l and set him on the ground. They laughed as the puppy staggered around and tumbled over his own feet.

"He don't look hardly old enough to be away from his ma yet. You sure he can hold off Indians, Sam'l?" Nathan laughed as the puppy sat down and yawned.

"If he grows into those feet of his, he can take on the whole tribe by himself. He's got feet bigger than the rest of him put together. He'll be fine once he gets used to using his own legs for a change. I been carrying him ever since I left the Fort early this morning."

"You must be hungry, Sam'l. This rabbit's ready now," Sarah said.

They sat around the fire on logs that Sarah had pulled up and ate from the lopsided bowls that she had carved during the evenings. She was pleased that they had proper dishes and spoons to use, even if they were rather rough. She had learned as she worked, and the last bowl was almost even. Sam'l was eating from it. The puppy nudged Sarah for another scrap from her bowl.

"Way he eats, he'll grow to his feet in no time," she laughed. "He needs a name. We ought to call him 'Empty'."

"What's the news, Sam'l? We ain't seen a soul since we left the Fort. How're the folks back there making out?"

"Well, James and Martha send their greetings, as does Jane Schmidt. I think Jane has a liking for you, Luke."

"I appreciate them remembering us," Luke replied.

"Except for that boy that nobody knows about and a few outlying families, most have gone back to their claims."

"Is that boy settling down some?" Luke asked.

"Not much. But the Indians seem to be. Most of the folks that returned to the wilderness felt that the raid where we got most of the captives back would show the Shawnees we mean to stay here and won't put up with their burning us out and their raiding our camps. It's been quiet since then."

"Do they know where the Indians are camped?"

Sam'l replied, "Scouts say that they went up north to that camp called Chillicothe. Heard that Tecumseh is trying to get the tribes together. He's got some good plans. We can live peaceably with the Indians 'long's he's around. He was gone to talk to some other chiefs when that renegade raiding went on 'round these parts."

Luke replied, "I heard that The Prophet, Tecumseh's brother, was the one behind the raids."

"That's true," Sam'l said. "He and Tecumseh don't see things the same way. I wouldn't feel as easy if the Prophet was in charge. I believe he'll be troublesome one of these days. There's more men than me that believe the same way."

Sarah listened to the conversation between Sam'l and her father. She felt very uneasy. Never as long as she lived would she ever forget the fearful time she had spent as a slave in the Indian village. She hoped the other captives had all been freed, but she was too afraid to ask. In his own time, Sam'l would tell everything he knew about it. He had what he wanted to say sorted out in his mind, and it would be rude of her to interrupt his thoughts.

Luke and Sam'l were still talking about Tecumseh and his plans to unify the Indian tribes when Sarah got her blanket. Sam'l had brought a haunch of venison with him. Partially soothed by the thought of meat other than rabbit or squirrel and the drone of the voices of the men, she fell into a restless sleep.

෧

The next morning, when Sarah had awakened, she unwrapped the venison from the skin of the deer. After the men had eaten, Sarah stretched the deer hide on a frame she had hastily made. Now, she looked for a good scraping stone. She scraped the skin as well as she could without weakening it to a breaking point. It would serve as a cover for one of the windows in the single-roomed cabin. There was no glass in the wilderness. The scraped hide would let in light, though she wouldn't be able to see through it. It would keep out some of the cold, as well. Later she told Sam'l, "Sam'l, I'm really thankful that you brought the meat and skin. Until Pa has the cabin built, he won't be able to hunt for deer."

Sam'l smiled, "You are more than welcome, Sarah."

"I also appreciate the chunk of salt with the meat. The salt lick is a full day's walk from here. We've been out of salt for a while now. Everything will taste better with some seasoning in it."

The men started to plan their day's work. It was time to get on with erecting the cabin. Sam'l, Luke, and Nathan were trying to see what to do next. Sarah, in order to stretch her cramped muscles, walked over to the garden plot. The beans were poking the first two leaves through the soil. She hoped they would bear well enough so that she could dry some for eating in the winter and, still have enough seed for next years planting.

The potatoes were in the ground. At the corner of the garden she had built a frame of poles. Pa and Nathan kept asking her what it was. They'd teased her about it, but she wouldn't tell.

She'd let them wait until they saw for themselves the surprise she had carried home.

Fondly, she looked at her father and brother. With Sam'l's help they would soon get the walls up for the cabin. Putting up the walls went quickly, and soon they would be started on the rafters. It would go much slower putting the shingles on.

"I wish I could help them," she said to herself. She could start by sticking small pieces of wood and pebbles in the cracks between the logs. Then when they started to fill them, that part of the job would be done. Sarah felt an unexplained loneliness. She was the only girl with three men. There wasn't anyone for her to talk to. She longed for another woman. Shaking off her feelings she pondered about how to plaster the clay into the cracks between the logs. Sarah could hardly wait to move into the cabin. It would be good to sleep under a roof again.

"Better get back to scraping. After scraping hides in the Indian village, I never thought that I'd look forward to doing that again. Guess that how you feel about something depends on why you're doing it," she thought.

At the cabin, Luke, Sam'l and Nathan worked without a need to talk. Each knew what must be done. Carefully, they notched the logs at the corners and fitted them together. It took all three of them to lift a log into place. Luke had been careful in his choice of logs. Those he had cut were not too heavy for the men to handle nor too small to make an unsteady wall. Luke had pitched the roof high enough to leave room for a loft during the winter. He was grateful that he didn't have to build another chimney. That was a time consuming and backbreaking job.

At the end of the day, they looked at the unfinished cabin. "I hope we can finish the rafters by tomorrow, Sam'l. You're a strong hand to have around. We'd be far behind without you," Luke said. "Let's go eat that meat Sarah's got cooking. I'm so hungry I could eat it raw tonight."

"I've got a surprise for you tonight," Sarah beamed.

119

"What you got, girl?" Luke asked.

"I went to the meadow and found enough wild strawberries for all of us to have a good handful. They sure taste good. There'll be plenty in a couple of days for you to get tired of eating them, Nathan."

Nathan grinned. "I could never get tired of strawberries. I wish they'd bear all summer. I'd eat so many that I'd turn into a strawberry."

"And you'd eat blackberries, and raspberries, and grapes in the same way," Sarah teased. "You've just got a hankering for sweets."

Luke cautioned, "You be careful going after them, Sarah. I don't want to have to rescue you from the Indians again. It wouldn't be as easy since you got away once, and now they won't trust you."

Sarah considered her father's advice and nodded her head.

"When it's time, I'm going to look for a hollow tree. Maybe there'll be bees in it. This year I'm going to beat a bear to the honey. When I find the honey, I'm going to sit down and eat a whole bowl of it," Nathan said, smacking his lips as he thought about the sweet, sticky, golden honey sliding down his throat.

"Don't you ever think about anything but eating?"

"Sure. Sometimes I think about drinking a cup of thick, cold milk." He smacked his lips again and leaned against a log.

"I declare, that boy ain't nothing but empty!" Sam'l laughed. "He's making me hungry and I couldn't hold another bite."

"Before we all starve to death listening to what Nathan'd like to eat, Sam'l, tell me what's happening at the conventions. I ain't had time to ask about that yet."

"It's mostly talk. James came back from Danville and said that there were men meeting there from every settlement in the country. Mostly, they were talking about being unhappy with Virginia. They don't like the idea of paying taxes to Virginia, and the laws they have in Virginia sure don't fit us here. Can't see why we should have to abide by 'em."

"What laws they referring to, Sam'l?"

"It's mostly laws and taxes that are for civilized places. We ain't civilized here in the wilderness. We should have laws that fit the wilderness. We shouldn't have to pay tax to support the cities in Virginia"

"Yep, I know. It's like the foolish law that says we can't chase the Indians across the Ohio River."

"Yes," Sam'l agreed. "It's like it was agin the law when we went over and got them captives back. I'd like to see one of them fancy dressed men from Richmond out here trying to keep his scalp. He'd sure change his thinking in a hurry."

"He'd change the thinking of some of the Indians, too," Nathan said. "I can just see one of them Redskins taking one of them fancy-men's hair and finding another scalp under the wig. He'd think the evil spirits had him."

"Luke, I declare, I ain't laughed so much in years. Don't know as I can stand much more," Sam'l chuckled at the picture Nathan's words had put into his mind. "That would be a surprise to any Indian. Speaking of surprises, I near forgot that Martha sent something for Sarah!" He rummaged in his pack and handed Sarah a small bundle. "Martha said you'd probably find a use for this."

Sarah cried out in delight as she saw a piece of cloth. "Why, it's the piece left over from the dress Martha made over for me when you brought us back from the Indian Camp, Pa. You remember how she ripped up one of hers to make it? She even sent a twist of thread. Now, I can put the first story of my life in Gramma's quilt." She hugged the cloth to herself and went to the lean-to. Tomorrow she would carefully fit the piece into one of the rotted out places. It was the beginning of a new life for her. It was a good omen.

CHAPTER FIVE

SARAH'S MISTAKE

"One more day should get the last of the shingles on. We've been lucky on the weather holding out. Don't like the looks of that ring around the moon. Might rain tomorrow," Luke said as they sat around the fire after they had eaten.

"Corn could use a good soaking, Luke," said Sam'l. "I just hope it holds off though 'til we finish that roof. The shingles you cut are a joy to work with. I've used some that weren't cut right on other roofs, and they made for a slow job. Ain't nothing slipshod about your work."

Luke nodded and accepted the praise from Sam'l. He knew he'd been careful cutting the boards for shingles. A man couldn't brag on his own work even when he knew he'd done the best he could. It was good to hear Sam'l say it.

"All that's needed now is to finish the roof and frame the window and the door. I brought some leather for the hinges. Its good buffalo, should hold up for years. Ain't no more buffalo in these hills. I got this leather from a fellow who was over the river last year. Said you could shoot any direction and hit a bull or cow. They were strung out far as you could see, he said," Sam'l remarked.

"I'd sure like to have one. It'll salt down good, and I'd like the jerky from it, too. Don't think there'll be time this year to go after one. There ain't no better eating than a roasted buffalo hump."

Sam'l agreed with Luke. They sat thinking about the great herds of buffalo that roamed the prairies. On a big hunt, the slaughter was unbelievable. Men shot the animals like shooting fish in a barrel. They took the hides and sometimes the tongues but left the rest of the carcass to rot on the prairie.

"Speakin' of salting down, Luke, I promised Martha I'd get her some salt from the lick, seeing as I was halfway there already. Usually, there's deer around the lick. I thought I'd shoot me a buck, but this time of the year it won't keep long enough for me to work it up. I been thinking. I could pack back the meat and salt, too. I'd obliged if you could spare Nathan for a couple of days. He could help me pack it back this far, and you could have half the meat. If you're willing, I'll take him along when we finish the cabin."

"That sounds good, Sam'l. We can use the meat. What do you think, Nathan?"

"Go to the lick with Sam'l? Oh, yes, I'd really like to go."

Luke said, "I'd go myself but there's so much to do here. Nathan ain't got a gun 'cause the Indians took the spare one we had when they took him."

"Don't matter none. It only takes one rifle to drop a deer."

"While you are gone, I'll split the boards for the floor. Nathan and I can peg them in when he gets back. We got all the pegs whittled so that won't slow us down none," Luke said.

Sarah had tried to make pegs, too, but, like her bowls, they were lopsided. She decided to concentrate on doing something she knew. She said to Luke, "Pa, tonight I'm going to make a basket. I got the white oak sapling split into thin strips, and I can weave while the rest of you talk. We will need baskets when it is time to gather the corn."

"Right, Sarah, that's mighty helpful of you."

"Luke," Sam'l interrupted, "I been thinking about that boy captive we got back from the Indians. Call's himself Little Deer and thinks and acts like an Indian."

"Yes, I remember him. He is staying with Martha and James isn't he?" Luke asked.

"Yes, and Martha has more than she can handle now with her own brood," Sam'l replied.

Nathan said, "I remember him. He hasn't got any idea who his family is. He has been with the Indians so long that he believes he is one of them."

Sam'l added, "He's a handful. He looks to be about eight, but he's plenty of trouble for Martha. She ain't complaining, but James said the boy leads her on a merry chase. She ain't said nothing, but James let it slip that there's another young 'un on the way. Martha don't need this kind of trouble right now."

"Are you sure he ain't Indian?" Luke asked.

"You ever see an Indian with blue eyes and yellow hair?"

"No, and I never hope to. Martha is such a good woman. Always did take on more than she had strength for. She's got her pride, too. How do you think you can get him away from her?" Luke asked.

"I don't rightly know. Don't know what I'd do with him, either, once she lets him go. Ain't many families left in the fort to take him on. Most of them are in the same fix as Martha. This boy needs a strong hand."

"Some of the children are afraid of him," Nathan said.

"Well, he is a trifle mean. He's played some mean tricks on other children. He tied little Anne Moore to a post and said he would hurt her if she cried. Poor girl was scared out of her wits."

"What happened to Anne?" Sarah asked.

Sam'l continued, "Matthew was passing by and cut her loose. Little Deer ran and hid under a cabin. He didn't come out till sundown. When he did, Matthew took him to the woodshed. He never let out a whimper, and I know Matthew left welts on him. The only thing he seems to take an interest in is his mean tricks."

"Do you have any idea of who he is, Sam'l?"

"Nobody 'round these parts knows of a family that might have lost a boy his age. All the people 'round here got their children back. James said he'd ask around at Danville. Maybe one of the men up there might know something. Don't know when James'll be back, or even if he'll know anything when he comes, but something's got to be done about the boy."

"I wish I could help Martha," Luke said. "She sure has been good to us. I just don't know what I could do, though. Let me ponder this situation. Maybe I can suggest something."

"If you do, let me know. Martha has been good to all of us at one time or another. There ain't a person in these parts don't owe her a debt of one sort or another."

"Well, the three of us do, for sure," Luke admitted.

"Guess we'd better turn in; it's been a long day," Sam'l said.

Sarah had listened and wondered what would have become of her if Pa hadn't rescued her and Nathan. She was older than the boy when she was taken and would have remembered her former life. But, she knew that in order to survive in the Indian village, she would have to adapt to the Indian ways. It must be frightening for the boy to be now in a white man's camp after being raised as an Indian. Troubled, she fell asleep.

ॐ

It was late the next morning when she awoke. She could hear the sounds of pounding coming from the cabin. What would the men think of her! She had slept past daybreak. She had had a restless night thinking of the child who didn't know if he had white or red skin. She felt sorry for him.

Shortly after noon, Sam'l and Nathan came up to the fire circle, where Sarah was working on her basket.

"Pa said he could finish the roof by himself, so Sam'l and I are going to the lick to get salt and a deer. Do you have any extra food we can take along, Sarah?" Nathan asked.

"I've got some strips of that meat that Sam'l brought; they're drying over there. It should be good enough to keep you going 'til you can get some fresh meat. Take the flint so you can strike a fire to cook it. I've got hot ashes, so I won't need the flint."

"Thanks, Sarah."

"I've also got some strawberries that I picked today. Just bring back the birch bark bucket they're in. I know your sweet tooth, Nathan. Just don't eat the bucket for the juice that's in it."

"Much obliged," Sam'l said to Sarah.

Nathan and Sam'l started off into the woods, heading in the direction of the salt lick. Sarah watched them go and marveled at how silently Nathan went through the woods. "Just like an Indian," she thought. They'd only been captives a short time, but they both had taken on some of the Indian ways. That's how it must be for the boy that Sam'l had talked about. He had been captured so young that the Indian life was all he knew.

That night, while she and Luke sat at the fire, she said, "Pa, why don't we tell Sam'l to send Little Deer out here? He could help you and Nathan clear the field. Maybe we could help him learn civilized ways again. He can't get into much trouble out

127

here, and there's so much to be done, he won't have time to get into trouble."

Little did she know how wrong she could be.

CHAPTER SIX

DIGGER

"That's a good buck, Sam'l. Dressed out real big."

"I can't take credit for it, Luke. Nathan got it with my gun—first shot, too."

"Nice going, Nathan. Well, that should serve our needs for a time. You ain't got your share. Take more than what you put in that pack."

"There's only me, Luke. I've got enough here to last me 'til I get out again. There ain't nothing to keep me housebound. That stew sure smells good, Sarah. What you got in it besides meat?"

"Well, I found some ramps. They're so strong, you have to watch and not put too many in. It does give the stew a good flavor."

"You sure know what to mix up to make foods tasty. All I do is roast the meat or make a simple stew. Guess you'll have to give me some cooking lessons."

Sarah laughed at the idea of Sam'l worrying about how to cook. As long as what he ate filled his hunger, he didn't seem to much care what it was or what was in it.

After Sarah had rolled up her blanket and gone to sleep, Luke and Sam'l talked about the boy who was causing so many problems for Martha.

"Sarah's willing for that child to come here, but I'm not sure she understands that all he wants is to go back to the Indian tribe. It's the only life he remembers. Our way of life frightens him, and he doesn't know how to act. He's more than I'd want to take on," Sam'l observed.

"Well, probably she thinks she can mother him. I guess she believes he'll be like a Ben—you know—a substitute for her little brother who was killed in the raid. I've heard her crying in her sleep and calling for Ben and Mary. It's like in her dreams; they've wandered off some place while she's supposed to be watching them. Then, she wakes up, and she's sad and quiet and keeps to herself—doesn't even fuss at Nathan about washing his hands. Lord knows, I miss them, too. I'll ponder about keeping him and let you know before you leave on what I've decided," Luke answered.

ॐ

The next morning, as Sam'l was getting ready to leave, Luke came to him and said, "I done thought it over, and I reckon we can give the boy a try. I'm not sure about it, but maybe it'll work."

Sam'l replied, "When I get time from my own claim, I'll go to the fort and get the boy. I'm sure Martha will agree to his going if she thinks it will help you. She knows that you have a lot of work, and the boy could learn to be helpful."

Sam'l said his goodbyes and started for his home place. Luke and Nathan started splitting the planks for the cabin floor. They started putting them in place right away, for everyone was anxious to move into the cabin.

The next day, it rained, a a slow and easy rain. Luke and Nathan were ready to bring the planks down from the woods

130

into the cabin. Sarah fretted at the delay. She was ready and wanted to move into the newly-built cabin.

"Pa, why can't we start carrying the boards down? We've been wet before."

"Now, Sarah, they won't peg proper if they're soaking wet. Wood swells when it's wet. The planks won't soak up as much rain there under the trees as they would out in the open. We'll get them down soon as it's dry enough to do a proper job. If we had iron nails instead of wooden pegs, it wouldn't be so tricky. But we ain't. You'll have to bide your time. Meanwhile, I'm going to work on smoothing that door. It's up at the cabin. Bring your basket and come along if you like. At the rate your goin' on that basket, it'll be ready for next year's crop 'stead of this one."

"Pa, I already made one. This is my second basket. I set the other one on the hearth. At least that was something I could move into the cabin."

Sarah sat on the stone hearth of the fireplace and worked on the basket. Luke had the door lying across the joists to which the floor would become attached. He stood on the ground between them and used them as a workbench. The oak door was still very rough. He pulled the drawing knife toward himself shaving off the rough places. It was slow work. Oak was very hard wood, but it made the best doors.

"Pa, we'll need shelves on that wall, and there should be some pegs under them. We won't be needing the beds built 'til I can get enough skins and corn shucks to make mattresses. I'm hoping you'll have time to fix us a table soon. Sitting on the ground to eat just don't seem right."

"I know, Sarah. Don't know how much time we're going to have. With the rain, the weeds'll be springing up in the corn. Somebody will have to hoe the corn. The crop comes before fancy fixin's. I ain't been tending to the corn like I should since we've been working on the house."

"We need to clear that new field, too, Pa. If the corn grows good this year, we'll be lucky to have enough to get us through the winter. Even at that, we'll have to be sparing of it." Nathan looked up from the handle he was making for his axe. As much as their axes were used, he was surprised that the handles had held out as long as they had.

"I don't even like to think about more chopping, but we're going to have to build up the woodpile before winter. Never know what the weather will be around here. I don't aim to go clear to the woods for a log every time we need one. Just makes good sense to have plenty of wood handy in case of a big snow."

"Do you think we can get the loft floored for the boy to sleep on?" Sarah's mind was filled with no thought of anything but the cabin. Later, she would think about the gathering of food for the winter. Right now, she was so pleased with being under a real roof with the rain pelting down on it that she didn't even care to think about food. She could imagine things in their proper places on shelves and pegs. She pretended the floor was already in place. "Pa," she said, "I'm going to sweep and scrub it every day until the floor is white and smooth, just like Ma did with the first cabin floor."

"Oh, Sarah, you are so busy in your mind! It plumb wears me out."

"Amen to that," Nathan added.

"In the fall, you or Nathan can shoot a turkey. I'll make fans out of the wings. We can use them to fan the fire hotter, and sweep the ashes away from the hearth, too. Pa, could you also shoot a bear?"

"Oh, Lord, child." Pa sighed.

"Then, Pa, I could make a warm cover for the bed out of the bear skin."

Later, as she watched Pa clear another field, she hoped to plant flax. She could make a loom just like Martha's and weave enough cloth for their needs. Maybe sometime Pa would take her to the fort so she could tell Martha how nice she had fixed the cabin.

"Sarah! I've called you three times. You sure are wool-gathering."

"Oh, Pa! I didn't hear you. I was thinking about the cabin and what was needed for it."

"I 'spose you've thought up enough to keep Nathan and me busy doing nothing but making your wishes come true." Luke laughed and shook his head. "You get more like your Ma every day." Luke turned his head to hide the pain he felt at Elizabeth's loss. "Your Ma would lay awake nights thinking up ways of keeping me busy so she could make things nice."

"Gramma always said the devil finds work for idle hands. Guess Ma just wanted to keep you out of the evil ways," Sarah teased.

"Well, I've got my hands full enough to keep two people busy, so don't go thinking up any more for me to do for a while."

"Or for me, either," Nathan added. "Pa, I'm going to sharpen up these plow blades. The rain's letting up enough so we can work outside. Being cooped up under a roof's bad enough in the winter without adding summer to it, too."

"Nathan, you'd probably live in a hollow tree if you had your way. You'd rather be outside than anywhere else. I declare, I believe you're turning into an Indian."

"Well, that ain't all bad," Nathan mumbled.

"That reminds me," Luke spoke up, "just because the Indians are supposed to be on the other side of the river don't mean there ain't none about. Don't know if they'll ever raid hereabouts again or not, but we need to stay watchful."

"I wish I had that old rifle back that the Indians took," Nathan said. "I wish we had one each for both you and Sarah to use when we're in the forest or the fields."

"I do too, Pa, but I don't think I could shoot at an Indian."

"Maybe if they was going to kidnap you again, Sarah," Nathan said.

"Well, the dog will be a big help, Pa. I'm teaching him to bark when you and Nathan come up."

"It will be a while 'fore he's good for anything but digging holes. I'm beginning to think he is more of a gopher than dog. He sure is a digger."

"Nathan, I could hug you! You just did it. You solved my problem. I've thought and thought, and you did it without knowing it."

"What are you talking about, Sarah? You been out in the sun too long?"

"You gave me the name for the puppy. We can't just call him 'dog'. It's the best name for him."

"What name?"

"Digger! That's his name now. It sure does fit him."
"Digger ain't no name for a dog!"

"It is now! What do you think, Pa?"

"Please, let me out of this argument."

Sarah smiled, "You might as well get used to it. Come on, Digger, the rain has stopped. Let's go look in the garden so I can teach you what you're not supposed to dig up."

CHAPTER SEVEN

FEATHER

"Pa, I'm going to go up to the clearing to pick berries after I finish washing these clothes." Sarah paused in her stirring of the garments boiling in the big, iron kettle that hung over the fire outside the cabin. She pushed back loose strands of her golden hair with her forearm and straightened her tired back. "Oh, Lord, I would like to rest, but the berries are ripe. By tomorrow, the birds will have eaten most of them."

"Now, Sarah, you keep a watchful eye out. Take the dog with you," Luke cautioned.

"He is too much of a puppy yet. I'd take twice as long if I took him. I'd have to chase him to keep him from chasing all the rabbits and squirrels. No, I'll leave him here and pick as fast as I can. I'll be careful, Pa. I don't ever want to be captured again."

Late in the afternoon, Sarah finished hanging the last shirt over the bushes to dry. She was tired from washing clothes, carrying them to the creek to rinse them, then wringing them out by hand and carrying them all the way back up the hill to hang them out to dry.

She'd had to tie Digger to a tree. He wanted to play tug of war with the clothes that Sarah shook straight before she draped them over a bush.

The kettle, having been cleaned and rinsed free of soapy water, now contained a stew that also enticed Digger with its odors.

Sarah decided to leave him tied until she returned. The puppy in him probably would get him into trouble if he were loose.

Her dress had faded to a dull color from many washings and age. Her hair escaped from under the cloth she had wrapped around her head to keep the perspiration from dripping into her eyes. Washing clothes was hot work. She wished she were as fresh-smelling as the clothes she hung, but she would wait until after she picked the berries to clean up. She knew that her arms would itch from contact with the leaves, and she knew she would be hot and sweaty again.

She picked up a basket and trudged toward the clearing where the berries grew. "I'm so hot and tired. I wish I could just leave the berries until tomorrow," she said to herself. "But if I don't get them now, we won't have any. Nathan loves them so much. I'll just pick what I can and hope there'll be some left tomorrow."

She reached the patch and began to pick. Her back ached so badly that she had to stop often and straighten up. If she could just lie down flat for a few minutes and stretch out for a minute, she thought, "I'll feel better, and I can pick faster," she rationalized aloud. So she lay down.

It felt so good to lie flat on the ground. Her tired muscles relaxed and her eyes drooped shut. She drifted off into a light, soothing slumber. Her body, covered as it was with the worn dress, seemed to blend into the ground on which she lay.

Slowly, she began to waken. She didn't want to move. Only her eyes opened, and she lay without movement, watching an eagle soar over the clearing. Sarah was lost in her own thoughts, watching the eagle, noticing that he was so graceful and so free. She wished she could fly and see what he saw from the sky. The eagle glided lower and lower, his majestic wings riding the air currents.

Suddenly, there was a whirring sound and a sharp 'whack' sound. The eagle stopped mid air, pierced by an arrow, folded his wings, and plummeted to the ground on the other side of the clearing.

The sight of the arrow brought immediate panic to Sarah. She clasped her hands over her mouth, stifling a scream. She had the presence of mind to remain motionless. From her position, she could see the edge of the woods. From it came an Indian dressed in shabby skins. He glanced around and ran for the bird. He held his prize high, and Sarah got a full look at his face. "Oh, my God, it's Running Deer!" her mind screamed. "What is he doing here?"

She froze. Memories of being dragged by him through the woods, living as a slave, being chosen to be his wife, and escaping from the Indian camp flooded through her. In an absolute panic, she pushed her body even closer to the ground. Then, as quickly as he had come, he was gone.

She lay immobile, waited, and watched. There was no sign of him. Cautiously, she raised herself so she could see all around her. She had to cross the clearing to get to the cabin. What should she do? She began to tremble. She was so scared.

There was movement again where Running Deer had disappeared. Relief flowed through her tense body. "Nathan! Nathan!" She tried to stand, but her legs wouldn't hold her.

"Sarah, are you here? I can't see you," he called.

The sound of his voice gave her strength. She ran across the field, berries forgotten, calling to him. He rushed toward her, realizing that something terribly frightening had occurred. They met where the eagle had fallen. Nathan held her shaking body as she poured out the story about Running Deer.

"Sarah," Nathan reassured her, "You were asleep and dreaming. You were lying on the ground. I couldn't even see you when I looked for you. You just had a bad dream."

After a while, Nathan almost convinced her that she had been dreaming. "You were so tired," he told her, "you just fell asleep. Let's go home. You can pick berries tomorrow."

ॐ

The next morning, when Sarah awakened, she thought about the incident with Running Deer. She knew he had shot the eagle. She decided to go and pick whatever berries were left. As she walked by the place where she thought the eagle had fallen, there, on the ground, was a bloodied eagle feather.

A sharp chill ran down her spine. She picked up the feather. "Oh, Lord, it's true, after all. Running Deer was here." She began to tremble and ran back to the cabin. "Now Nathan and Pa will know I wasn't dreaming. Running Deer is alive, and he's on the loose!"

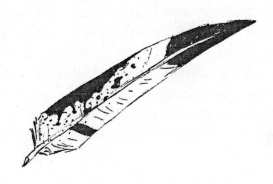

CHAPTER EIGHT

LITTLE DEER'S WELCOME

It was coming into early summer and the corn was beginning to tassel. Soon, the ears would form. Luke had planted some pumpkin seed in the cornrows, and the vines were hanging heavy with bright, yellow-orange blossoms. Sarah had picked and strung beans up to dry. The strings hung down from the rafters of the loft. She loved to look at them, knowing that next summer she would produce all the beans she could use. All that she allowed herself to cook this year was one small potl of green beans. She had transplanted wild onion shoots to her garden and was waiting for the bulbs to grow large enough to dry. They would keep well and be good to eat during the winter.

After Luke and Nathan had put the floor in the cabin, there were three boards left over. These had been laid up in the loft, but that was as far as they had been able to get with the flooring of the loft.

The blackberries were ripening, and, as she picked them from day to day, she dried some. The berries were spread on the boards in the loft; Sarah hoped to cover all three of the boards with drying berries.

Luke had set a board across two fairly large log,s forming a makeshift table. Come winter, he thought, he would have time to build a trestle table and benches, but for now the boards had to do. He had cut a maple tree from the new field, and now it was seasoning. When it dried enough, he would make the table and benches Sarah longed for.

As for Sarah, she had pulled the bark from the logs they had used to sit upon at the cooking fire. These served as stools for them now. Sarah tried to make a three-legged stool, but, like her bowls, it was lop-sided and a bit dangerous. The only thing it could be used for was to hold the water bucket. Even then, the bucket had to be set on the stool a certain way or the whole thing would fall over. When it actually did spill, Sarah laughed and said that was one way to get the floor washed.

"Pa, do you think Sam'l will bring the boy back?"

"I don't rightly know, Sarah. Does it bother you?"

"Pa, I just ain't sure. Since I saw Running Deer, I been mighty scared again."

"I know, Sarah. I don't know if or how Running Deer got out of the stockade. But it's worrisome for me, too."

Later in the day, Sarah went to her trellis at the end of the garden. Pa had laughed at her "surprise" seeds when they had begun to grow. "So that's your surprise! Just like your Ma," he said. "She was bound to have gourds, too."

Sarah was careful to keep the young gourds off the ground. She was going to dry them to make dippers and pots to hold the seeds. If they lay on the ground, they bruised and would rot before they could dry. She tied them with bits of grapevine. Digger's favorite place to take a nap was under the gourd trellis. Try as she might, she couldn't keep him from there. Finally, she used sticks to make a rickety fence around it. Pa had called it "Sarah's Folly."

She was boiling clothes in the kettle at the side of the cabin when she heard Digger barking. Quickly, she ran into the cabin and closed the door as Pa had told her to do. Her heart seemed to freeze within her. "Please don't let it be Indians," she prayed. "We're just getting started again." She crouched down behind the door and trembled, but she was proud of Digger's warning. That dog was making enough noise to be heard clear over the mountains to Virginia, she thought.

"It's all right, Sarah. You can come out and get this critter quiet. He's learning good." Pa called out to her. "It's Sam'l coming back."

"Is the boy with him, Pa?" she called in a frightened voice.

"Can't rightly tell. Looks like he's dragging something on a rope. He's behind some thick woods now. Should be coming into the open pretty soon."

"You did a good job, Digger." Nathan bent over to pat the dog. "You ain't much for size yet, but if you grow as big as that bark of yours, we can hitch you up to a plow and save us a lot of back-breaking work."

"Come on, you varmint!" Sam'l gave the grapevine rope a tug as it tightened in his hand. "You gave me enough trouble getting you here."

"Sam'l, what on earth do you have? Where's the boy?"

"At the end of this rope!"

"You tied him? Like an animal?" horrified, Sarah ran toward him.

"Watch out, Sarah. There's no telling what he'll do. He's a wildcat. He's bit me, kicked me, and clawed at me 'til I feel like I crawled into a cave with a mad she-bear. I don't know that I'm doing you right by bringing him here."

Pa and Nathan stood with their mouths agape.

"Oh, that poor little boy. How'd you expect him to act, tied like that? I know what it feels like to be dragged through the

141

woods at the end of a rope. It ain't a nice feeling." Sarah rubbed the scars on her wrists where the rope had cut her when she had been tied by Running Deer when he had captured her. She would bear the scars for the rest of her life.

She knelt to untie the rope from the boy's wrist. "I'll bet your hair's real yellow when it's clean," she said as she reached out to take a leaf that had become tangled in it.

She pulled back in horror as the full, hate-filled glare of his blue eyes met hers. Prickles of fear ran down her spine.

What had they gotten into?

This was foolish, she decided. Firmly, she said to Nathan, "Take him to the creek and give him a good scrubbing. He's not coming into my house that filthy."

"I'll go with you, Nathan," Sam'l said. "It'll take one to hold him while the other scrubs. I had to drag him out from under a cabin where he had been hiding. Martha tried to wash him, but he kicked her so, she couldn't do it. I'm so put out with him, I've a mind to hold him under the water 'til he gets some sense."

"It's a good thing Sarah isn't going to scrub him; he wouldn't have any skin left on his body," Nathan laughed.

Sam'l dropped his pack, and, taking a firm grip on the child's arm, led him to the creek.

"Pa, maybe I was wrong. I ain't so sure bringing him here is a good idea," Sarah said.

"Well, he is here. Just give him a little time, Sarah. He'll come around. He just ain't used to our ways yet. Maybe giving him a bath ain't the right way to start out."

"As dirty as he is, I wouldn't even want him in the lean-to. He smells like a polecat."

"Sounds like one, too," Luke said as they heard the wild, splashing sounds coming from the creek.

"Wonder why he don't yell?" Sarah questioned.

"It ain't the Indian way. That's what he's been raised to think he is. We must remember that, Sarah, and make allowances for him."

Sarah went back to her steaming kettle to finish her washing. When she had hung the wet clothes on bushes, she started roasting the quail that Nathan had killed that morning. Since the weather was so warm, she cooked on a fire that was built outside.

"You sure were gone a long time," she said to Nathan and Sam'l as they came back from the creek. The boy limped between them. His blond hair sparkled golden in the sunlight. How could this little boy, who looked like the picture of an angel, be so much trouble?

"Do you want some blackberries?" she held the berry-filled birch bucket out to him. "I know you're hungry. All boys stay that way."

The child ignored the bucket as though it weren't there.

"Patience, Sarah," Pa said. Sighing, she set the bucket on the stoop. If he wanted the berries, they would be there. She went into the cabin.

She could hear the voices of the men as they talked. "Guess Pa's finding out all the news of the fort," she thought as she went about her work.

"I'd better turn that meat. Almost forgot about it with all the excitement. Ugh!" Sarah pulled her bare foot back in disgust as she stepped into the sticky mess on the stoop. There, mashed into the stone, were the blackberries she had left for the boy to eat.

"That's the limit!" she fussed while she cleaned up the mess. It'll take a week of rain to get the stain out. I ain't goin' to put up with it. He'll have to learn how we live—and fast."

The boy was nowhere in sight, but she could hear voices coming from the cornfield. She started for it. To get there, she had to pass the bushes where the clean clothes hung. Suddenly she stopped. Big blobs of mud had spotted them.

Sarah was furious. Each step she took as she walked toward the field increased her anger. "Where is he?" she cried to the men, who stood there looking at the growing crop.

"Who?"

"That boy!"

"I thought he was with you in the cabin. I saw him go inside," Luke answered.

"Well, he ain't! But he sure did his dirty work."

Quickly Sarah told them about the berries and the clothes.

"He's run off again." Sam'l decided. "I'm about ready to just let him go."

"Now, Sam'l, we can't do that. It's just going to take time," Luke said. "Come on, we'll go find him. He can't have gone far. Where do you reckon he'd head?"

"North, most likely. He's trying to get back to the tribe. Sometimes, I'd just as soon he would. I wonder why we ever brought him out. Guess that yellow hair and blue eyes had us fooled. He's as wild and untamed as he can be. Mean, too."

They started into the woods after the child. Nathan stayed with Sarah.

"Oh, Nathan, I could just cry. It ain't because I've got to do the washing over. I just feel in my bones we made a big mistake. We're going to have trouble over him. What did Sam'l say they called him?"

"Little Deer."

"That's an Indian name. What's his real name?"

"Nobody knows, Sarah."

CHAPTER NINE

THE GIFT

Sarah, Sam'l, Luke and Nathan sat around the board that they used for a table and ate their meal. The child crouched in a corner. He would not sit with them. Sarah had fixed a bowl of food for him. It sat on the floor in front of him.

"Pa, it's worse than feeding Digger. At least he eats what's set out before him. We can't let the boy starve."

"He won't starve. He'll eat when he gets hungry enough. Just pay him no mind. He ain't used to our ways and, 'though he doesn't know it, he's embarrassed. Don't look at him. Act like he's not even here. He'll come around. Patience, Sarah. You can't change him overnight," Pa lectured.

After they had finished their meal, Nathan, wrapped in his blanket, curled up against the wall. He was tired from pulling tree roots from the new field and had fallen asleep. Luke and Sam'l were sitting on the stoop outside the door and were talking. Sarah had taken their bowls and was washing them. Slowly, the boy's hand reached out and picked up some meat that lay in front of him. He stripped the meat from the bones and threw them on the floor. His hunger satisfied, and realizing that he was trapped in the cabin, he curled up like a puppy and went to sleep where he lay.

Sarah came into the cabin. "What a mess he's made again," she thought. She looked down at him. He looked like a cherub, curled up asleep. He must be exhausted to sleep so hard. Carefully, so as not to wake him, she spread over him a skin that Sam'l had brought. Then she picked up the bones and threw them out for Digger to chew on.

Digger growled as she put the bones before him and wouldn't touch them. "Guess you smell a stranger on them. Come on, Digger, eat them. They're good bones." In the morning, Sarah found the bones untouched by the dog.

Sam'l was getting ready to go back to his place. "You done good, Luke. Don't know as I'd have had the spirit to go on after losing what you did. I wish you luck with the boy. If anybody can win him over, you can."

"I just hope that Sarah can tolerate him. She sets such store by that cabin. If he does anything to really rile her, I feel sorry for him. She's got a temper, though she don't look it. She knows right from wrong, and with her there's no middle ground."

"Well, the men ain't back from Danville yet, so I still don't have no more news about where the boy came from. He's been with the Indians a long time. I hope we can find his kinfolk. Maybe he'll be better off with them than troubling you all."

Sam'l turned to Little Deer, looked him straight in the eye and said, "Little Deer, you mind these folks. They'll treat you good. Don't do any more foolishness."

Little Deer sat passively, but his eyes were on Sam'l. For some unknown reason, Little Deer seemed to like Nathan. When he saw he couldn't escape, he gave up trying to run away. At least he stopped sneaking away every chance he had to try to get back to the tribe. No one knew for sure if he was just waiting for a better chance, or if what Sam'l said really made a difference.

Splitting logs was a two-man job, so Little Deer was left pretty much to himself. He had Luke's knife and was crouched over a long stick, whittling a sharp point on the one end of it. When he had the stick cut the way he wanted, he gave the knife back to Luke and walked into the forest.

"Do you reckon he's running off again, Pa? Should I go after him?"

"No, Nathan. Let him go. We've got to show him that we have trust in him. That's been part of the trouble so far."

"What do you mean, the trouble so far?"

"We don't chain the dog," Pa replied. "How can we chain the boy and expect him to act human? I've been as wrong as anybody else about him, but when he ain't looking at me, I've been watching him. Did you ever see the look in his eyes?

"No, Pa, I ain't been looking at him that much."

"The look in his eyes puzzled me 'til I remembered the time when I saw a wolf in a little pen. The boy's eyes looked just like the eyes of the wolf in that pen—scared. He was a wild critter, in a little cage he couldn't hardly turn around in, lookin' at strange people poking and prodding at him. I reckon Little Deer feels like a trapped wolf, 'cause I see real fear in his eyes."

The boy was gone for about an hour. So quietly did he return that Nathan and Luke didn't realize that he was back. He squatted near a stack of cut boards and, with a strange and satisfied look on his face, watched them at their work.

Screams split the air. Luke grabbed his rifle and headed for the cabin. Something was terribly wrong for Sarah to scream like that. Since he hadn't heard Digger bark, he knew that it wasn't Indians. What could have set her to screaming that way? He ran faster.

Sarah stood at the cabin door. Her hands covered her ears, and her eyes looked wildly at the still squirming rabbit, pinned to the floor by the spear that Little Deer had made. Squeaks that were growing fainter came from the mouth of the rabbit. Its blood was spreading in a pool around him staining the freshly washed, still damp floorboards.

"Stop it, Sarah! Stop it this instant!" Roughly, Luke shook her. A light stinging slap stopped the screams. She turned to Luke and buried her face against his chest. Deep sobs jerked from her throat.

"Oh, Pa! Oh, how could he? He ain't even human! Torturing that rabbit like that! What'll that varmint do next? Pa, get that rabbit out of here."

"Take it easy, Sarah."

"I don't think I can even look at it again. I was emptying the water from washing the floor, and I saw Little Deer sneaking out of the cabin. I knew he'd been up to something with his crafty ways, but I never expected this."

Unnoticed, Little Deer had come up to the cabin in time to hear Sarah's words. His shoulders sagged as he turned away and limped back into the woods. He was confused again. Sarah cooked the food he ate. The rabbit was his way to do his part for the family. He would never understand why Sarah had been so upset. An Indian woman would have been pleased with the meat and proud of him for spearing the rabbit through the back of the neck. No organs had been pierced. The flavor of the meat would be better than if he had broken the insides. It took skill to hit a running rabbit as he had done. Little Deer wouldn't make the mistake again of bringing Sarah a gift. She didn't know how to appreciate it. All she cared about was scrubbing and cleaning. His eyes narrowed. He'd make sure she got plenty of that to do, then she would be pleased.

148

CHAPTER TEN

SAM'L BRINGS NEWS

"**S**arah, I've made up my mind to give you a rest. Tomorrow, I want you to fix a packet of food for Nathan and Little Deer. I'm going to send them down to the creek to fish. I'll stay here at the cabin with you. They'll be told to stay 'til dusk. The signs are right for the fish to be biting, so that should keep them busy. If they have a good catch, we'll dry some fish for the winter."

"That's good, Pa. But how do you figure sending them fishing will give me a rest?"

"You ain't thinking, girl. Little Deer will be gone and out of your way the whole blessed day."

"Oh, he ain't so bad, Pa. It's just the tricks he plays. The only thing he ain't bothered is the gourds. I guess that's because Digger stays by them so much. The dog sure don't like Little Deer, and Little Deer keeps his distance from the dog. I declare, that dog is the only one around here the child fears. Maybe if I bit a plug out of him, the way Digger did, he'd do better for me, too."

"Just have patience with him, Sarah. He's just a little boy, and he's been acting better since you let up on scrubbing the hide off him every time he turned around. Indians don't set as much store 'bout washing as you do. Keep reminding yourself he's been raised different. Our ways are as strange to him as his are to us."

"I just wish he'd learn not to stick his dirty hands in the pot where I'm cooking and eat from it. That reminds me, I have to whittle another bowl. One of them is gone. I looked everywhere for it, and I can't find it. It don't seem likely that I misplaced it. Everything we got is in plain sight."

Sarah looked around the cabin. There wasn't much to see. The shot mold and her knives, flint, bowls and spoons set upon the shelf by the door. Pa's rifle hung over the fireplace. The big, iron skillet hung on a hook nest to the stone chimney. In one corner, the blankets and skins upon which they slept were neatly rolled. In another corner, the baskets she had made were stacked. Strings of beans and onions hung from the rafters of the loft, and along the wall under the loft hung the cleaned tools they had used. Next to the door was the wobbly stool she had made and the oak bucket that Pa had made for her one stormy day. In the center of the one-room cabin stood the board table with the log stools around it. On the table was the stone for grinding corn. In it was a small chunk of salt that Sarah had been breaking up. The missing bowl was nowhere in sight.

She had even climbed the ladder to look in the loft. All that she had found there were the baskets of dried fruit, some skins she had cured, and Gramma's carefully folded quilt. She was sure that the bowl was not inside the cabin. She'd look again outside. She didn't remember having taken it out, but she'd look to be sure. It wasn't that she'd done such a good job on the bowl or that there was much lost. It just bothered her to lose something needlessly.

"You'll find it, Sarah. It didn't walk off by itself. Just don't be wandering off thinking it's in the woods. I still ain't easy 'bout the Indians. It's time they go on a hunt again. It ain't likely they'll come this way for a while, but you never know what's likely with them."

"Then why are you sending Nathan off to fish?"

"He won't be alone. Little Deer will be with him."

"But, Pa, give Little Deer a chance and he will run off with the Indians."

"You might be surprised, Sarah. I hope the time don't come to prove me right or wrong. Little Deer took to Nathan right off. I don't believe he'd want anything to happen to him."

"He probably took to Nathan 'cause Nathan likes being dirty, too. He won't wash unless someone makes him either. I think boys were just born to be dirty. Here they come now, bringing some kind of mess with them, I reckon."

"Pa, look," Nathan held up a squirrel. "Little Deer showed me how to spear him just like he does. It won't be long until I can spear just as good as he can."

Little Deer looked at Sarah and from his mouth came the chattering sound of a squirrel. Frightened, Sarah covered her ears and ran to the woodpile. He sounded exactly like the Indian who captured her. She'd be glad to be free of him for one day. Every time she was beginning to feel that he was doing better, he did something mean to hurt her. She wondered if he'd ever be civilized and was eager for tomorrow to come.

Early the next day, Little Deer and Nathan set off for the creek. Sarah decided that it was time to start making moccasins to wear when the cooler weather came. She took a skin from the loft and went outside with it. Luke was working in the cornfield. Digger lay quietly at her feet. It was so peaceful. She let her hands lie idle and watched a bee flitting around the garden patch. She'd have to remember to tell Nathan to watch for bees. He'd follow them and try to find the honey. Soon it would be time to pick the pumpkins and dry them. The ground nuts would be ready. She could roast them in the ashes or boil them or fry them. They were just like the sweet potatoes they used to have in Pennsylvania. She wished she had told Nathan to bring back some cattails from the stream banks. She could grind the roots and use them just like meal. Soon the nuts would be ready to drop. They'd find plenty to eat. It had been a good summer. She grew drowsy and was almost asleep.

The hairs pricked up on Digger's back and a low growl started deep in his throat. Someone or something was coming. The dog leaped to his feet and began to bark. Luke came quickly from the field. A long "Hallo" sounded from the woods.

Sam'l was back. As usual, he brought something with him. In time, he would open his pack and bring out some kind of surprise for them. Sarah went to get him something for his thirst.

"This blackberry juice sure cuts the dust in my throat, Sarah. Didn't expect such a treat. I'd never think to squeeze the berries, I just pick them off the vines and eat them."

"It ain't hard to do. I mashed them with my grinding stone and strained the juice though a bit of cloth that Martha sent. It turned the cloth a pretty, deep blue. That will go so good on Gramma's quilt. The juice could do with a little sweetening, so if you make it, use some cane in it, or honey if you've got it"

"Sam'l ain't got no time for fancy fixings, Sarah. Only women take time for things like that."

"That don't mean it don't please me to enjoy it. You'll make some man a good wife, Sarah."

Sarah felt a new emotion. She felt her cheeks getting red. She had always liked Sam'l but knew he was many years older than she was.

"I ain't ready to take on a husband yet," she murmured.

"Well, you will be soon, Sarah," Sam'l said gently.

"Right now, Pa and Nathan are enough for me to take care of, and Little Deer is more than enough. I've all I can handle right here." Sarah looked down and thought, "If I do, I would want someone just like Sam'l."

"I got news about Little Deer. I'll tell you tonight so's I've only got to say it one time. Nathan'll want to hear it too. Don't know that Little Deer will be glad about it."

"Luke, let's go finish plowing that new field of yours. I get restless just sittin' when there's something waitin' to be done. That new field needs to be worked up so's it's ready for plantin' next spring. I know Matthew will be saving some flax seed for this fall. A field of flax will give Sarah something to do besides wear out the cabin's floor scrubbing it."

The men walked toward the field. Sarah smiled as she watched them go. That Sam'l was always finding something to tease her about, she thought fondly, watching them go. She wondered why he had no wife, but she supposed she'd never know. Sam'l never talked about himself.

She'd better start thinking about supper, she decided. Maybe, with Sam'l here, Pa wouldn't mind if she went for some ground nuts. She went to the field to ask him.

"Just don't go out of yelling distance, Sarah. They'd be good with the fish the boys are sure to be catching."

"I hope they're catching as many as you think they are. When I get back, I'll chop a whole rack of wood to dry all the fish we can't eat tonight," she commented.

"Oh, get on with you, Sarah. Sam'l sure brings out the smartness in you."

As she went into the woods, she thought about the flax field. She'd have to build herself a loom. It would be good to weave cloth. Their clothing was wearing out. Pa would have to build her a spinning wheel this winter. She would make the loom herself. She wouldn't trust that job to anyone else. She hoped it would be better built than her stool and bowls, and she thought about Sam'l.

CHAPTER ELEVEN

ABNER

Sarah had the cooking fire going outside. She raised up from the coals, where she had put the ground nuts to roast. It was getting late. The boys must be having good luck or they'd have been here before now; surely they wouldn't have stayed if the fish hadn't been biting. Fresh fish would taste good. There hadn't been much time to go fishing until today.

For supper, she planned to wrap the fish in leaves and steam them. "It would be better if I had some grease to fry them in," she thought.

Digger began barking. That must be Nathan and Little Deer coming, Sarah decided, and she started down the hill to meet them.

Proudly, they held up grapevines strung with fish.

"Oh! Just look at them all! They're beauties! Oh, Nathan, Little Deer, there are so many of them. Pa! Sam'l! Come see the fish!" Sarah was so excited that she hugged both of the boys.

Little Deer pulled back as she put her arms around him. He couldn't remember anyone touching him like that before. It felt curiously good, but he didn't know what to do. Somewhere at the back of his mind there was a dim memory of softness. He would remember the pleasant feeling and that Sarah liked the fish.

"Come up to the cabin. Let's get them cleaned and ready to cook." Sarah was so happy she didn't notice that she had hugged Little Deer again, as well as Nathan.

"Nathan, will you start another fire with green hickory wood so we can smoke the fish we don't eat?" In just a few minutes, Sarah was cooking the fish for the evening meal.

Sam'l was building a rack to hold the fish. Little Deer was sent to cut grapevines to lace across the rack and bark to cover it. Sarah gathered leaves and wrapped the cleaned fish. She added some of the herbs she had gathered throughout the summer. Luke continued cleaning fish.

"I declare, Sarah, you're bustling around just like Martha. I never saw a woman yet who couldn't put a man to work when he was ready to rest," Sam'l chuckled as he laced the vines on the rack he had made.

"Martha is a good woman. These fish need to be tended right now. In this weather, they'll turn rank before morning. They'll be good eating later on. No sense wasting 'em. The boys got more than we can eat. We don't waste nothin' we don't have to. We all did without much food last winter at the fort, and I don't ever want to be hungry again."

"Sarah, is your fish about done? Let's eat. I'm starved," Luke called. We can finish cleaning these other fish after we're fed."

They ate the fish until they couldn't eat anymore. The mounds of bones grew and grew.

"We can put these bones in the field, Pa. Indians plant fish with their corn." Nathan said. "Maybe they are trying to grow fish," Nathan laughed to himself. No one else did.

"Well, we'd better put them in the old field. The new field is going to grow flax. "Wouldn't it be better to put the corn in the new field and put the flax in the old field? Corn don't need that much tending. It could be farther out." Sam'l said.

"I didn't think about that," Luke answered. "Might be a good idea. We'll try it and see how it works."

"I heard that changing things around in the planting made them grow better. Don't know why, they just do."

"Speaking of growing, don't you think Little Deer is getting taller?" Luke asked.

"Yes, and by the way, I got news about him. James got back from the conventions. Even brought back a newspaper, the *Kentucky Gazette*. First newspaper in Kentucky. It told all about the goings on at the convention. Sure was good to see a newspaper 'though I couldn't make out all the words. Never did hold much with reading, but I wish I'd paid more attention now."

"You didn't happen to bring the paper with you, Sam'l?"

"Matter of fact, I did. Thought you could read, Luke. Maybe you can fill in the words I missed. 'Pears there's a lot of them." Sam'l was ashamed to admit that he could only read his name, little else.

"The paper will be handy. Nathan and Sarah ain't had no book learning since Lizabeth died, along with what little they got at the fort last winter from Frau Schmidt. I never even thought about it. Lizabeth set great store by reading—always said the only thing she missed out here was her books. We couldn't carry them with us; they were too heavy to pack. I can use the newspaper to teach them words. Might even get Little Deer started. He sure don't talk much, but maybe he will read."

"James said he met a man who knew something about him. According to him, he comes from reading people. Little Deer's name is Abner, Abner Peabody. He belonged to a family that lived about thirty miles east of the fort. They was raided about five, six years ago. His Ma and Pa was killed. They came from up east. There was a brother of his Pa's came out with them. He was from Boston. He went back there before they got raided.

"How can you be so sure that Little Deer is Abner?" Pa asked.

"Well, I don't rightly know for sure. This brother might know. He came out to see what the country was like. He was writing a tract about the new country. Some land company hired him to tell about how good it was. Anyway, one of the delegates knew about them, remembered the family and the little boy—blond, blue-eyed—who was never found. He said the baby had a birthmark like a strawberry on his chest and a foot that wasn't straight, same as Little Deer has. I saw the mark today when the boys came up from the creek. Guess they went swimming after they caught the fish. First time I ever saw Little Deer clean since Sarah had him scrubbed when he first came. I didn't notice the mark then, since I wasn't looking for it. Anyway, there's a letter on the way to his uncle telling him the boy is found. Frau Schmidt wrote the letter."

Luke stared at the ground and finally spoke. "I don't know if sending a letter is a good idea. What if Little Deer isn't Abner."

Sam'l, noting Luke's resistance, continued, "No doubt this uncle will want to come out and see if Little Deer is Abner. If he is, he will want to take him back to Boston. I'm pretty sure I met the uncle once. Think his name was Henry. He didn't seem like the type to come to the wilderness, but he seemed to set great store by his family. He'll do what he should about the child. He won't be able to get here until next spring, though. It's too dangerous to try to get through the gap through the mountains in the winter, and he ain't the kind to do anything foolish.

158

Little Deer had listened intently to all that Sam'l had said. He wasn't sure of what Boston was, but he knew he wouldn't like it. When he had a chance, he would ask Nathan about it. He could talk to Nathan. Little Deer was very afraid of what would happen to him.

Luke's heart sank. He knew that Little Deer had been trouble, but he felt a strange pull to the mixed-up child. He had hoped that they could keep him. He had grown to love the half-wild little boy. He wanted a little brother for Nathan. He wished that Sarah could take to him more.

Sarah was glad that Little Deer would at last have a home with his own people. He belonged with them. Let them try to tame the savage that he had become. She was tired of fighting with him. She worried about how it would be when they all were shut up together in the cabin in the winter. "I'll be glad when you are gone," she muttered to herself.

CHAPTER TWELVE

SOUR NOTES

"Pa, does Little Deer really have to go away? Couldn't we keep him? He'll hate living in the city. I wouldn't like it myself. He'll fret himself to death."

"I don't like it any better than you do, Nathan, but we ain't got a choice. That uncle of his is his blood kin. If he cares enough about the boy to come way out here to get him, he has a right to him. He'll not let anything happen to him. We'll just wait and see. Likely, Little Deer's uncle ain't even got the letter yet. We'll worry about losing Little Deer when the time comes to worry. Until then, we'll just go on like we have been. Don't go borrowin' trouble, Nathan. There's plenty of it around without having to go looking for it."

"I guess you're right, Pa. Is it all right with you if I take Little Deer to the creek? I can talk to him there. He's got that wild look about him again. I know he's scared, but he'll die before he says so."

"You're the one he's latched on to. It'll come better to him hearing it from you. Remember now, nothing ain't for sure yet. We don't even know that his uncle's still in Boston. First thing in the morning you two go on to the creek. Be back when it's

161

noon, we need to get the corn in. Now go up to bed. Sarah's already gone in."

Little Deer had heard enough from Sam'l to make him edgy.

Sam'l came to the fire. He pulled a white bundle from his pack. "Here, Luke, I almost forgot this. Martha sent it for Sarah. She'd have my scalp for sure if I carried it back to the fort."

"What is it?"

"I don't know. Some kind of woman's trappings. Looks like a big sack to me. Martha said to tell Sarah she wove it from the flax that James grew. She said it was good and strong. I 'spect Sarah'll know what to do with it."

"Why don't you give it to Sarah yourself? She'd be pleased."

"I ain't goin' to be here that long. I'm planning on leavin' 'fore sun-up."

"I hate to see you go, but I know how it is when you got places to go. It pleasures me to have a man to talk to sometimes. There ain't nothing to talk about 'cept crops and work around here. Sure is good to hear what's happening other places."

Luke and Sam'l sat and talked until the fire was nothing but a bed of red embers. Then they, too, went to sleep.

౨

In the morning, when Sarah woke, Sam'l was gone. Folded next to her was the present that Martha had sent. Sarah squealed with delight when she unfolded it. Bundling it in her arms, she ran outside to Luke. "Look, Pa, Martha's sent a mattress cover. I'm going to stuff it with corn shucks today. I won't need to wait till we have enough skins to make one. Now all I need is for you to make the bed for me to put it on." She was so excited she could hardly talk.

"Whoa, Sarah. First things first. Don't you think it would be best if we got corn in and shucked before you started stuffing mattresses with it? That'll be in the fall. Anyway, today, we've got smoking fish to take care of. You wouldn't want that nice clean cover to smell like fish, would you?"

Luke watched her go into the cabin to put the cover carefully away. It took so little to make her happy. He'd get to making that bed first chance he had. For now, though, he'd better start cutting the weeds out of the corn. He wondered how Nathan was making out trying to explain to Little Deer about his uncle. Wonder if Indians have a word for uncle, he thought.

Down at the edge of the stream, Nathan sat whittling on a reed. Little Deer watched him and wondered what he was making. He really didn't want to hear what Nathan was saying. "City? What is a city? Boston was no tribe he had ever heard of before. 'Pa' was what Nathan and Sarah called their chief. Little Deer wondered, "What does all of this have to do with me?"

"Little Deer, you're not listening. I'll try to explain it in a different way." Nathan picked up a stick and began to draw pictures in the dirt. First he drew a picture of a man

"This here's your Pa. And this is your Ma." He drew a woman.

"Chief. Squaw." Little Deer pointed to the figures.

"All right, we'll do it your way. Chief. Squaw, Papoose. Papoose is Little Deer many moons ago when Little Deer was named Abner Peabody."

"Little Deer name Little Deer, not what you say," he interrupted.

"Now it's Little Deer, but then it was Abner," Nathan insisted.

Little Deer shrugged. He knew his name. Let Nathan call him whatever he wished.

Nathan rubbed out the dirt figures of the man and the woman and drew several Indians around the baby.

"Shawnee come. Raid. Scalp Pa and Ma. Take Papoose."

Then he drew a village and put in it a little boy dressed as an Indian. "Now, Abner is Little Deer."

Little Deer grunted agreement. "Little Deer!" he pointed to himself.

"Now, Chief's brother comes to take Little Deer to his village, Boston."

"Where that?"

"Far over the mountains toward where the sun rises." Nathan explained.

"That not Shawnee."

"No, Little Deer. It's a white man's village."

"Little Deer no go!"

"Not right now, no. Later. Many moons from now. After the big snows. This is good medicine for Little Deer."

"Little Deer no go," he repeated firmly, but the fear was still in his eyes. He went off to the side of the bank. He didn't want to hear any more.

"I wonder if he knows what I tried to tell him. No telling what he's thinking." Nathan picked up the reed and began whittling again.

Little Deer stared into the water. He knew he looked different from the other Indian children, and he limped, but he was treated the same as they were. He knew he didn't have a mother and a father. That was not unusual. Many braves were killed and many squaws had died. Their children were taken in and made a part of another family. He'd never thought about it before, now he was forced to. He didn't want to leave here unless he could go back to his tribe.

Nathan was his friend—no, his brother. They had made a pact. They had cut their wrists and held them together so that their blood mingled. Now they were brothers. Sarah was just like a squaw—always jabbering about something to which he paid no mind. She fed him good food, as she was supposed to. He did like to come up behind her and smell her hair. It had a pleasant, woodsy smell. If she caught him at it, she got angry with him. Still, he did it because he liked to. He wasn't sure how he felt about Luke.

He hadn't figured Luke out yet. Sometimes he was a strong chief. At other times, he did as Sarah said. No Shawnee chief let a squaw tell him what to do. Little Deer would decide about Luke later. He knew that what Sam'l had talked about concerned his future. If Sam'l said it, it had to be bad. He didn't like Sam'l. He stayed as far from Sam'l as possible. Never would he forget Sam'l's dragging him through the woods. Little Deer was not a dog to be tied. His eyes narrowed. Someday he would tie Sam'l and drag him through the woods, he promised himself. An Indian never forgot a wrong. He'd get even, though it took years. His thoughts were disturbed by reedy sounds coming from Nathan. What was wrong with his brother? He ran to him.

"What you do?" he asked.

"I made a flute."

"What flute?"

Nathan showed Little Deer the stick that he had been whittling on. "Well, you blow here and put your fingers here. When you blow, you get different sounds if you lift your fingers.

165

See?" Nathan blew into the flute and made some sounds come out. "Here, you try it."

A thin, high-pitched squeal came out as Little Deer blew as hard as he could.

"Not so much air. Just easy. Do your lips funny, like this." Again, Nathan showed Little Deer. "It takes practice. Here, this one's yours. I'll make me another one."

Nathan began whittling another flute from a reed.

Little Deer sat on a rock and blew into the reed until his face was red.

"You're trying too hard. Blow easy."

Soon Little Deer was able to make the sound less like a screech owl and more like the sounds Nathan made.

"You work at it. You'll be able to play music in no time."

"Sun up over our heads," Little Deer said.

"Time to go back. I'm glad you saw it, Little Deer. I wouldn't want Pa to think I was trying to get out of work. We got to get to the corn field and help him."

Carefully, Little Deer carried his flute back to the cabin. He hid it in a special place he found between the floor and the wall. There were other treasurers of his there.

CHAPTER THIRTEEN

ANOTHER GOOD HUNT

"It's about to frost. Seems like the summer just flew by. Sarah, so if you've got anything growing that you want, you'd better get it up. It'll freeze in the next two or three days. Looks like we're in for a long, hard winter again this year."

"How do you know, Pa?"

"Well, the corn shucks were heavy and the wooly worms have thick coats. That means a hard winter. I been counting the days since I heard the first katy-did. It'll frost ninety days from then. I got eighty-seven marks on the wall. We got three days at the most to go. Could have been a katy-did sounded before I paid it any mind."

"When it frosts, I'm going to turn over my gourds. I can't pick them until December or January when they're good and dry. I'll need to slice and dry the pumpkins, too. We've been eating them pretty fast. Pa, do you suppose we can get any maple sugar this year? I wish we had some sorghum. That'd be good."

"We ain't got a sorghum mill. It takes a horse or mule for that. Sure wish that horse we brought with us when we came here hadn't been taken in the raid. We could have made good use of her. Her colt would have been big enough to be a help, too, if we had it," Luke said, matter-of-factly.

"I know, Pa, I wish we had the horse, too," Sarah said sympathetically. "The nuts should be ready to gather soon. They'll taste good this winter when meat is scarce. Pa, for a long time I ain't had no fat for soap making. I need fat to make enough soap to last through the winter."

"I don't know why you'll need so much. Nathan will use very little." There was only a little smile from Sarah. Luke continued, "I been thinkin', Sarah, we need salt, too. That last salt Sam'l brought us is about used up. We're going to have to salt down some meat against a big snow like we had last year. I guess I'll have to go to the lick and get us a supply. Maybe a wild boar, too. That would give you plenty of fat for soap, and the meat's as good as tame pig."

"If you got one big enough, I could render down the lard, too. It'd be good to have something to fry things in. If I had some flour, I could make a pie. I guess I could grind up some cattail roots and use that. A cobbler would taste good. I could use some of that dried fruit, or maybe make a persimmon pie if it freezes hard enough before they are gone."

"Oh, Sarah," said Luke, "that brings back memories. I ain't had a pie since Lizabeth made one. Seems like an age ago. I'll see what I can do about getting the pig. I ain't going to leave you here alone. I'll need one of the boys to go with me. Who'd you rather have, Nathan or Little Deer?"

"Need you ask? You take Little Deer. Nathan and I will be fine."

"You ain't got no rifle. I don't like leaving you that way," Luke said.

"I'd rather be here with Nathan and no gun than with Little Deer and a whole room full of rifles. He gives me the whim-whams," Sarah said.

"All right. Soon's it frosts, I'll take Little Deer to the licks. We'll see what we can scare up in the way of meat. I don't like to go, but I don't have much choice. It's a good day to get there, walking hard. If we get meat, we'll have to pack it back in stages. May take up to a week to get back."

"Don't worry about Nathan and me. We'll be fine. There's plenty to do to keep us busy while you're gone."

"I just wish you had a rifle. I'm uneasy. The Indians have been too quiet."

"Now, Pa, Sam'l said they was in a big pow-wow. They had a pow-wow when we was in the village. They talk until all of them are heard. It's just the Indian way. I know how long it takes for just a few of them. If what they're talking about is big, it may take all winter before they decide what to do. Well, I know what I have to do tomorrow. I'm going to bed now." Sarah curled up in her blanket. Soon they would need more cover than one blanket each, and it would be cold sleeping on the floor of the cabin.

It was late when Sarah was awakened by strange sounds coming from the creek. No noise like that ever came from a frog. She lay half-awake, listening. She'd never heard sounds like that before. She wondered what it was. She was too tired to get up. And she drifted off into a deep sleep. The noise was curiously soothing. It made her think of Ma singing lullabies to her when she was small.

◌

Luke and Little deer had started toward the licks at daybreak. It was late afternoon when they got close.

"Little Deer, when we get closer start looking for rub signs or acorns that look like they've been riled up. There'll be game," Luke said as they neared the salt lick. "There should be some deer around there. Most of all, I want to get a pig for Sarah. It'll take a while to pack the meat we get back to the cabin."

169

At the lick, they cut several chunks of salt and settled back to await the return of the animals they knew would come. Luke had told Little Deer they would take no does. Little Deer had his spear and Luke carried the rifle. Patiently, they watched. Two does came into view. Luke signaled Little Deer to wait. Finally, a big buck appeared. Little Deer was excited. Swiftly, he launched his spear. It grazed the shoulder of the buck, and he and the does ran off. Little Deer was unhappy. He had forgotten the first lessons of patience he had learned. He had thrown his spear too soon. Luke would be disappointed in him.

"It's all right, Little Deer. You just got too anxious," Luke said as he patted him on the shoulder. "The buck won't be back for a while, but there'll be more tomorrow. We'll get one then."

Why hadn't Luke punished him for being so impatient, Little Deer wondered. "A brave on a hunt would be very angry with me. Punish me. I no understand Luke," Little Deer thought.

They rolled up in their blankets they had brought and went to sleep. In the morning, the deer would be back.

ॐ

The next morning, Little Deer was awakened by a shot. He sat upright quickly. "Little Deer, come quickly, and bring the knives." Luke called.

On the ground lay a big buck. Little Deer was again ashamed. He had slept until the sun was up. Luke had killed the deer while he slept. Silently, he helped Luke dress out the deer and prepare it to carry back to the cabin.

"It's best we eat before we hunt anymore. I'm going to cook some of this liver. It will take a while. You go see what you can find that will go with it." Luke told Little Deer.

Still ashamed, Little Deer wandered into the forest. He stopped under an oak tree. The ground was roughed up under it and rooted up. It looked like wild hogs had been there. He

170

remembered Sarah talking about boars. He'd track them and get one for her, he decided.

Carefully, he studied the spoor. It hadn't been long since they'd been there. He followed the broken bushes. His nose picked up the stench of pigs. Now he would prove himself.

Suddenly, he tensed. He was in danger. A sow shot out of the brush. Her tusks were dripping with saliva. She charged him.

"Pa! Pa!" he screamed. The wild pig came at him, her breath rancid in the air. Little Deer saw the charge and jumped to the side. She raked his shoulder with her tusks, and he fell to the ground, bleeding, as she prepared to charge again.

A shot sounded and the sow dropped to her knees. Another shot and she was still. "Stay back, son, don't go no closer. She may not be dead."

Carefully, Luke went up to the sow. "Watch out for her mate. He may be close. If he smells her blood, he'll be meaner than sin," Luke warned. Luke approached the pig and cut her throat.

"You get a vine and we'll string her up. She's too heavy to move, so keep an eye out for danger."

They tied her by her front legs and hoisted her up into a tree. Luke slid his knife down through her belly and cleaned out the carcass. As the heart was cleared from the cavity, Little Deer caught it and swiftly cut a slice from it. He stuffed it into his mouth and chewed it, the blood running down his chin.

"Indian warrior eat heart to get strength back," Running Deer said to Luke.

Luke nodded. He knew that Little Deer must eat the heart of the animal he had just killed. If he didn't, he would be afraid and cringe in fear when he saw another animal.

Little Deer didn't like the taste of raw meat. He knew he had to eat part of the heart raw or he would become as a woman. He reflected on just what had happened. "Luke saved my life. Now my life belongs to Luke," he thought. "Our spirits are joined until I save Luke's life. Then the debt will be repaid." He knew that he was Luke's, body and spirit.

Luke came to where Little Deer stood fanning the fire to get it blazing to heat the stones for cleaning the hair from the pig. "You're hurt, Little Deer. I thought the blood was from the pig. Let me look at your shoulder. That's a bad gash. We'll have to clean it out. It ain't going to be easy. Pigs ain't the best thing in the world to fool with. They'll eat anything. No telling what you got in that wound from her mouth. I'm going to hurt you, son. I don't mean to, but it will hurt."

Luke washed the wound with salty water. It was deep and bleeding. Luke gathered a handful of spider webs from a nearby tree and laid them on the deeply gashed shoulder. Still it bled.

"I'll have to burn it to make it stop bleeding," he said. It'll hurt like fury. Can you stand it?"

Little Deer looked at Luke. "Yes, Pa," he said. It was the first time he had ever spoken directly to Luke, and the "Pa" was music to his ears.

"That's my boy," Luke said. He took his knife and heated it to red hot in the coals where the liver was cooking. "This'll hurt," he said as he took the knife and laid it across the open wound. A sickening smell of scorched flesh rose from where the knife met the wound on the child. Little Deer clamped his teeth together, tightened his lips, and never uttered a sound. He felt sick to his stomach from the pain, but he would not make Pa ashamed of him again.

CHAPTER FOURTEEN

SARAH'S SURPRISE

Sarah looked up from the pumpkins she was slicing to dry on the vine laced racks. Digger was barking. Frightened, she ran into the cabin, and watched from the doorway.

"It's all right, Sarah," Nathan called to her. "It's just Pa and Little Deer coming back."

"It's too soon for them to be showing up. Are you sure, Nathan?"

"Yep. See for yourself. They're breaking though the woods right now."

As they came into the clearing, Nathan and Sarah could see that they were dragging something behind them. Curious, he ran to meet them.

"What you got there, Pa?"

"It's something Little Deer rigged up to haul the meat. The Indians use these when they're moving. It's a good thing to know about. Look at it."

Nathan examined the two long poles. They were lashed together with vines and held apart with a shorter stick at the ends that Luke held. The farther ends met and crossed each other where they trailed on the ground. On the bed formed by the laced vines lay the meat and salt that Luke and Little Deer brought with them.

Sarah came toward them. "What's happened to Little Deer's shoulder, Pa? It looks like a bad wound." She bent to look more closely but stopped when the child pulled back. His eyes warned her not to touch him.

"Sarah, we got you enough pig fat to make all the soap your heart desires. Brought a big chunk of salt, too. We can salt down plenty of meat with it. Nathan, did you get that oak barrel built to hold it?"

"Sure did, Pa. It's as tight as I could make it. I used willow to hold the oak staves together. It's a good, stout barrel."

"The meat's dressed out and ready to cut up. There's plenty of skins to keep you out of trouble for a while, Sarah. I thought to try to smoke one or two of the hams from the pig. Sam'l told me about his tasting it and he said it was good eating. It's some new fangled idea from Virginia. Some settlers coming in told him about it. They had some ham with them, and Sam'l said it was right tasty. I get tired of dried and salted meat all winter, and I ain't going that far off to hunt again for a while.

"What did you bring back, Pa?"

"We got two pigs and a buck. Little Deer got the shoat with his spear. He's a tough little guy. Didn't let that bad shoulder hamper him none at all. Never let on that it bothered him. He's good on the trail, too."

Sarah didn't want to listen to any more of Pa's bragging about Little Deer. "Let's get started on that meat before it turns bad. Nathan, you fill the big kettle and get the water boiling. We got to scrape the hair off them hogs."

"We dug a hole in the ground and filled it with water and put in some hot rocks. Then we dipped the hogs in it and got most of the hair. It won't be too bad, Sarah," Luke said.

174

"Well, it'll still take scalding water to get off what you missed. Wish I could have got them soon's they was killed. It would have been easier."

"I can just see you, Sarah, going hunting, dragging your big kettle with you," Nathan said, sarcastically.

"I'd just as soon you'd shot them around here, Pa. It's best to get to them soon as possible." Sarah ignored Nathan.

"I didn't have a choice, Sarah, I had to hunt them where they were." Then Luke told about the sow's attack on Little Deer.

"Don't know as I could have taken you burning my cut to stop the bleeding without passing out," Nathan said. "Little Deer, you sure are brave."

"We'd better stop talking and get to the meat before it spoils." Sarah didn't want to hear any more about Little Deer. "If he'd stayed with Pa, like he was supposed to, he wouldn't be hurt. Then Pa could have waited to get the pig right around here so's it could have been tended to proper," she grumbled to herself as she went to get the knife.

After their hides were scraped, the pigs were hung from the tree branches, where Sarah cut fat from the carcasses. This would be melted down until it became lard. That job could wait until the next day. Luke and Nathan cut up the meat and stacked it on rocks. As soon as they finished building their smoke house, the meat would be ready to go on shelves in it. Little Deer had been sent to cut the small logs for the smoke house. It wouldn't take long to build. No chinking was needed between the logs so that the air could get through. They should have it ready by evening. It was cold enough now. The meat would keep.

As the carcasses were cut apart, Sarah trimmed up the meat and rubbed salt into the pieces. Some of the trimmings would be chopped up fine and mixed with herbs she had gathered and dried during the summer. This sausage would be fried and packed in its own grease. They could take out as much or as little as they needed whenever they had a hankering for sausage. Later, the grease would be used for soap making.

The middlin' meat would be salt-cured and used for bacon. She planned to cook the ribs for supper and pack in grease what was not eaten. Ribs wouldn't keep as long as the sausage. Digger would be in a heaven of bones until all the ribs were eaten. The hams and shoulders, packed in a thick blanket of salt, would wait on the shelves in the smokehouse until spring, when they would do the smoking of them as Sam'l said.

The buck was tended to next. Now they had enough meat to last them through much of the winter. For a change, they would piece it out with the rabbits and squirrels that lived in the forest near their cabin. Sarah looked up from the meat she was working on.

She saw that the poles were in place for the walls of the smokehouse. Nathan was handing bark shingles up to Little Deer on the roof. Pa was splitting boards for the shelves. The shed was very roughly made, but it didn't matter. It would serve its purpose.

She went back to cutting the meat until it was as fine as she could get it. At last, she was satisfied with it. She put down her knife and went into the cabin to get the herbs for the sausage.

As her eyes got used to the change from the sunlight, she noticed a skin-wrapped bundle on the board table. She peeled back the covering and, shocked, drew in her breath. There, in the skin, was the head of the pig. Its eyes were open and seemed to look back at her. Sarah's eyes grew wider and wider.

"Drat that boy!" She picked up the skin and, holding the head as far from her as possible, threw it out of the doorway of the cabin. It landed at the feet of Little Deer.

He looked at Sarah and thought, "How can girl be so stupid? She not know the head is best eating." He shrugged his shoulders and kicked the head aside. He should have known that Sarah never knew what was good. "She is stupid, stupid, stupid," he murmured to the trees.

CHAPTER FIFTEEN

THE LETTER

"Pa, something's been in the honey. I been noticing it going down awful fast. Nathan said the last time he dug the honey out of the trees, he'd starve before he'd get stung like that again. Don't know as we'll get any more unless you rob the bees the next time."

"He did get stung awful bad. He sure was a sight with his eyes swelled shut. Only good thing about it was that you kept him plastered with mud. He never thought the day would come when you'd plaster mud on him. He said it was almost worth the pain."

"Well, it kept the hurt down. Mud is the best thing for bee stings there is, Pa."

"I think Nathan was kind of upset when he couldn't find any more stings to put mud on. He had to start washing himself again."

"That still don't tell me where the honey is going. Honey's the best sweetening we got. The dried berries sure taste good when I can cook them with honey."

"You keeping the lid tight on the honey bucket? Might be some varmints getting into it."

"Pa, that lid's so tight I have to use both hands to pry it off. It's a varmint all right. I just ain't sure which one. When I catch him, I'll show him what honey's good for."

"Now, Sarah, you saying it's one of the boys?"

"I ain't saying for sure 'til I know for sure. I just believe that varmint has got two legs."

Luke and Sarah were in the cabin. Outside, they could hear the sounds of axes biting into wood. It was cloudy, and the smoke was slowly rising from the chimney. That was a sign of snow, Luke had said, and he had the boys getting plenty of wood split and piled close to the cabin.

Sarah was working on the dried gourds. She held up the dipper she had just finished. "Look, Pa, it turned out good. Guess I'm better with gourds than wood. Now I'm going to make a ladle to dip out soup and stew."

"You got enough gourds fixed to hold seeds. You could put one seed in each gourd and still have some empty ones," Luke teased.

"Oh, Pa, they're good for holding more than just seeds. It's a good thing that you built me another shelf." She had a satisfied feeling as she looked around the cabin.

Luke had built the bed in the corner, and Sarah had laced the frame with grapevines to hold the mattress that was stuffed fat with corn shucks. Over the mattress was a blanket and Gramma's quilt. The quilt was still missing some pieces, but Sarah loved to look at it.

Nathan had built a bench that sat next to the fire. Little Deer had watched Nathan work, and one day he came in with a three-legged stool—like the one that held the water bucket—but Little Deer's stool didn't wobble. Sarah sat on it now as she worked.

Luke was building a trestle table. Since they were crowded in the cabin so much because of the cold, the board table had been knocked over many times as they moved about.

Digger's bark warned them that someone was coming. Luke lifted his rifle down from over the fireplace and went to the door.

"Pa, it's only Sam'l," Nathan called and went to meet the man as he came to the clearing.

"Come in," Luke welcomed Sam'l. "Drop your pack and tell me what brings you out this far at this time of the year? Didn't expect to see you until spring."

"Hello, all. I got news for you. A fur trapper came by and gave me this letter. It's for you."

"A letter?" Sarah was excited. "I've never seen a letter before. What does it say, Pa?"

Luke carefully opened it and puzzled over the writing. "Don't know as I can make it all out, Sarah. It's been through some hard weather, and I ain't too good at reading writing," he admitted. "Let me study it out."

Little Deer and Nathan came inside. "It's starting to snow, Pa. Looks like this could be a big one. If you can help us, we'll get the wood up to the cabin. We've got a lot split. Looks like we might be needin' it all."

"Sarah can help," Sam'l said, winking at Sarah.

Sarah, embarrassed, looked down at the floor.

Sam'l got up and went outside with the others. With the four of them doing the carrying, they soon had a good pile stacked next to the door of the cabin.

"What you got to eat, Sarah?" Luke asked as he shook the snow from his shoulders. "It's getting bad out there. Looks like we're in for a long snow."

"We got plenty to eat and plenty to do. It won't be all that bad," Sarah said. "Not like the last time. There's rabbit stew cooking in the kettle. Get your bowls. I've got cornbread in the skillet. We can't keep the snow from coming down, but we sure can eat."

They sat around the board table, except for Little Deer, who squatted in his usual place on the floor.

"See you ain't tamed him yet, Sarah," Sam'l said.

"Well, he's learned to wash," Sarah answered. From the way Sam'l smelled, he could do with a washing himself, she thought, though she didn't say it.

After supper, they sat around the fire inside the cabin. Sam'l pulled his pack closer and opened it. They never knew what he'd bring next. This time, he pulled out a bearskin. "Got her on a hunt last year. I got all the skins I can use," he said as he spread the fur on the floor.

"Oh, Sam'l, it's beautiful and so soft. The boys will be warm under this up in the loft this winter." Sarah ran her hand over the fur.

"I'd kinda thought it would keep you warm, Sarah," Sam'l said.

"Oh." Sarah felt a twinge of excitement. "But, I got my blanket and Gramma's quilt. I can snuggle into the mattress. It's Pa I'm worried about."

"The next bear skin I get goes to him, Sarah."

"That would be good, Sam'l, because now all he has is that blanket we brought with us. He rolls up in it before the fire, so I know he won't freeze. He should build another bed, but he says we don't need it. We need the room more than another bed. Guess he'll have to do something if it turns real cold. That floor is drafty."

"Your Pa knows what's good for him, Sarah." Sam'l turned to Luke and asked, "Did you read the letter yet, Luke?"

"I think I know what it says. I puzzled it out while you were stacking wood. But to be sure, Sarah, get the letter from the shelf and read it to us."

"It's from Henry Peabody. His writing is cramped and hard to read. Part of it is water-spotted and there's folds where I can't read."

"Just do your best, Sarah."

"Henry says he is the brother of Abraham Peabody who was killed in an Indian raid. He tells about the child named Abner that was taken by the Indians when he was three years old. Henry is sure that Little Deer is that boy. He's coming to get him as soon as he can get through the pass.

"The part that is hard to read," Sarah continued, squinting a bit as she deciphered the inked scrawl, "tells about the boy . . . blue eyes, something 'e-r-r-y' mark. That's in the fold. I can't read it. There's about two lines I can't read, then 'foot'. There's something about his foot. Then he writes about his brother, Adam, and his sister. I can't make out her name.

"Anyway," she concluded, "he's comin' and Adam is, too. Guess you'll have to build another bed, Pa. This Henry don't sound like the type to be happy sleepin' on the floor. He'll want a bed. 'Til he comes, you can use the time to get it ready for him. You got all that seasoned wood in the loft."

"I find this whole thing troublesome. Right now, I'm not thinking about anything but getting some sleep." Luke got his blanket and rolled up in it before the fire. Sam'l joined him. The boys climbed the ladder to the loft.

Rolled in their blankets, Luke and Sam'l talked. "Do you think this Henry can get anywhere with Little Deer?" Sam'l asked.

"I don't rightly know. It depends on how he strikes him at their first meeting. Little Deer sets a lot of store by how he feels at first about someone."

"Guess that's why he goes out of his way to stay out of my way," Sam'l admitted. "I shouldn't have tied him to bring him here. Guess I got off on the wrong foot with him. He just fretted me so, I didn't know what else to do. I been trying to win him over ever since then, but I ain't had no luck."

"He's getting civilized. Nathan says he talks to him a lot. When the sow gored him, he called me 'Pa'. It was the best feeling I've had in a long time. Sarah's the only one here that won't accept him as he is. I think she'd like to, but she just don't understand him and won't take the time to try. I don't understand her. She knows what it's like to be a captive of the Indians."

Little Deer felt Sarah's rejection and so made no attempt to talk to Sarah.

CHAPTER SIXTEEN

LULLABY

They were kept in the cabin for three days because of the heavy, constantly falling snow. The five of them were crowded into one room.

Sarah felt as though she couldn't breathe. The air was stale and smelled of wet leather as the men tracked in and out with wood. Even though they went just outside the door, it was snowing so hard that they were covered with it. The floor was tracked with the melting snow from their clothes. She'd never get the floor clean again, she thought. As she tried to go about her daily chores, one or another of the men or boys was constantly in her way.

Luke and Sam'l accepted the snow as something that kept them inside, but it would pass. They set about finishing the trestle table and made benches to set on either side of it. Each of them was smoothing a bench. The sound of the drawing knife scraping down the length of the board grated on Sarah's already tight nerves. The benches stuck out into the room, and she had to go around them as she went back and forth from cooking the stew in the fireplace. Wood shavings littered the mud-stained floor.

Nathan was working on a moccasin. He sat on the floor near the fire. Bits and pieces of leather were scattered about him.

Digger had been allowed inside because of the heavy snow, and his damp fur reeked of a wet dog odor, while his thumping tail dried the mud into a small whirlpool of rising dust.

Little Deer just sat. His eyes seemed never to leave Sarah as she worked. This bothered her more than the clutter and the dirt. If she didn't get out of this cabin soon, she would scream. She couldn't stand it another minute. Taking a skin from the pile in the corner, she headed toward the door.

"Where do you think you're going, Sarah?" Luke looked up from the bench.

She pulled the skin across her shoulders and said shortly, "Out!"

"You can't go out in this snowstorm. You get two steps away from this cabin and you can't tell where you are. We've had to hang on to the walls to get to the wood. Now, come back and sit down. Here, try this bench and see how it feels to you."

"Oh, Pa, I've got to get out of here before I bust!" She let the skin fall to the floor and walked over to the bench. Luke put his arm across her shoulder.

"It ain't going to snow forever, Sarah. Patience, child. The worst is over. At least, we have plenty of food in the cabin to last us, and we're all well. It's going to let up today. I can tell by the way the wind's blowing. You're tired and fretting over the mess. Why don't you curl up on the bed and sleep a bit? You'll feel better."

"In the middle of the day? I ain't sick."

"You're goin' to make yourself sick if you keep on like this. Go on now—get up on the bed. You'll feel better if you rest a little."

Sam'l smiled at Sarah and nodded.

Sarah did as she was told. Little Deer watched her. He knew just how she felt. He climbed the ladder to the loft and went to the wall where he had hidden his treasures. Sitting there in half-darkness, he took them out one by one. Finally, he found the reed flute that Nathan had made for him. He stuck it into the front of his shirt next to his skin. It made him feel better having it there. The voices of the men came to him from the room beneath.

"What do you think is going to come out of the conventions, Sam'l?"

"I ain't sure, Luke. Now they're talking about maybe Kentucky separating from Virginia. That seems to be the most popular plan. There's some other plans, too."

Nathan quietly got up from the floor and climbed to the loft. He got his blanket and rolled up to sleep. He didn't even notice Little Deer sitting near the wall.

The men continued talking about the conventions. Little Deer paid no attention to their words until he heard the word "snow". Then he began to listen again.

"I'm grateful you got housebound, Sam'l, even if it ain't too comfortable for you. I miss talking to a grown man. It wasn't so lonely for me out here when Lizabeth was alive. I sure do miss her. I guess I especially miss her singing as she went about her chores. She had the prettiest singing voice I ever heard. She used to sing in the choir in church when she was a girl. I know she missed her music. Back in Pennsylvania, we use to sit around the fire after supper. Lizabeth would play her autoharp and sing. I sure would like to hear music again. Don't guess there'll be any music out here for a long time." Luke sat in silence and stared into the flames.

Then he shook his head and said, "I'm sorry, Sam'l. Guess I should keep my feelings more to myself. Here I am tiring you talking about Lizabeth. I ain't talked to nobody about her since she died. I shouldn't wear you out with my thoughts of loved ones who are gone."

"Luke, every man loses someone he loved. There comes a time when he has to talk about it to a friend. I'm glad I am your friend."

Luke got up and went to the door. "Snow's letting up, Sam'l. It'll be good to get some fresh air. Let's go outside and take a look."

The two men left the cabin. Up in the loft, Little Deer thought over what he had heard. As he thought, he felt the reed flute that was still inside his shirt. Carefully, so as not to waken Nathan, he climbed down from the loft. Opening the cabin door, he stood at the entrance and saw where the men had pushed through the snow toward the smokehouse. He supposed they had gone to check how the remaining meat was. They would be there for a while. He was sure they would take the time to cut off a frozen section of meat to bring to the cabin. That was slow work.

Little Deer struggled through the deep snow toward the edge of the forest. He swung himself easily up into a low, snow-laden tree until he was seated in its crotch. Then he pulled the reed flute from his shirt and started to play upon it.

A strange but soothing sound came from the forest toward the clearing. Luke and Sam'l looked up from the meat they were cutting. Puzzled, they looked at each other.

"Must be Nathan playing, Luke. You said you wanted music, now you got it. I saw him foolin' with a reed flute the last time I was here."

"He don't play that good. Sounds just like the wind blowin' through the branches. Maybe he's been practicing. Funny, I never heard him at it."

"Well, he must have practiced an awful lot. It sure sounds good."

Little Deer finished what he was playing and climbed down from the tree. He had the flute stuck safely again in the front of his shirt. He was coming back to the cabin from the woods when Luke and Sam'l came out of the smokehouse.

"Little Deer, did you hear the music? Luke asked.

"Music? What is music?" Little Deer asked with a puzzled voice.

"You know what music is. It's . . ." Luke couldn't explain what music was to Little Deer. "How do you tell someone what music is, Sam'l?"

"Beats me, Luke."

CHAPTER SEVENTEEN

TIME TO LEAVE

"You boys go somewhere. Go up in the loft or go outside. Let me get the floor cleaned up. It's the biggest mess I've ever seen." Sarah shook her broom at Nathan and Little Deer. "I want to get it clean before Pa and Sam'l get back from the woods."

"Come on, Little Deer, let's go down to the creek. It's too cold and snowy to fish, but we'll be out of the way. It ain't safe to be around Sarah when she gets the cleaning bug biting her. We can break the ice and bring back some water for her. That'll save her having to melt snow for cooking and cleaning." Nathan pulled his buckskin shirt over his head.

"Why don't you go help Pa and Sam'l bring down the wood, Nathan?" Sarah asked.

"I reckon they'd like to be rid of us all for a while. It ain't often Pa gets to talk man talk. Sam'l's leaving in the morning. There's no telling when he'll be back. Probably not before that uncle of Little Deer gets here from Boston. We ain't going to bother them, Sarah. Men need to get off to themselves sometimes."

Little Deer and Nathan left the cabin to go down the hill. Little Deer begged, "Nathan, please, we go to my tribe. Sarah no want us here. We go?"

Surprised, Nathan answered, "Oh, no, Little Deer. We aren't Indians. We can't go to your tribe. It just won't work. I know how Sarah acts toward you, but we can't go."

Little Deer walked with his head down. Finally, he said, "Much snow."

"It's going to be gone soon. It sure was deep for a while. The way it's warming up, it should be melting some today. We better stay out from under the trees. When the snow gets wet from melting, it gets heavy. Might break off some branches. I don't want no tree limb falling on me."

At the creek, they cleared off a rock and sat down on it. Little Deer pulled out his reed flute from the front of his shirt and began to play sorrowfully on it.

Nathan sat looking at the trees that leaned out over the stream. The white branches were heavy with snow. The trees seemed to be like very old, gnarled men with long white beards hanging from their bent heads. They looked like old Prophets from the Bible stories Gramma used to tell. He wondered what tales these old trees would have if they could talk.

Little Deer was thinking, too. Last night, he had listened to Luke and Sam'l talking about him and his leaving here. Now he understood that Boston was a very large village with many wigwams close together and many people. There was no place to hunt. The man who would come for him was not like Luke or Sam'l. He was not a woodsman. He was a teacher. Little Deer understood that he was not a teacher like the old chiefs who sat around the fire and talked of many things while the young braves and boys listened respectfully. Little Deer knew that he would not like this man. He had made up his mind not to go with this brother of his father. If he stayed here, he would be forced to go. He must run away. Even if Nathan wouldn't go, he would go as soon as possible. He would miss Nathan, his brother, the most. But Nathan would understand why Little Deer had to run away. Luke had been kind to him and had saved his life. Little Deer said to himself, "I will come back some day and repay my debt to Luke."

He knew that Sarah would be glad he was gone. He also thought, "Sarah not like me. She get happy with me gone. I try to make her happy with gifts. She only get angry with me. Maybe she get happy with my last gift."

"Little Deer, I've called you twice." Nathan shook Little Deer from his thoughts. "It's cold here. We'll freeze. Let's go back to the cabin and get warm."

Little Deer stuck his flute back inside his shirt and took a long, last look around. Then he followed Nathan up the hill to the cabin. Each carried a pail of water. Smoke curled lazily from the chimney.

When they opened the door they were met with the mouth-watering smell of deer roasting and the clean odor of the soapy water with which Sarah had washed the floor.

"Clean your feet before you come in," she called to them. "Little Deer, go back and shake that snow off your moccasins."

Yes, Sarah would be glad when he was gone, Little Deer decided.

"Where were you boys?" Luke asked.

"Down to the creek getting some fresh water for Sarah, Pa. How come you and Sam's are back already? Thought you were getting wood."

"Too dangerous. Branches falling everywhere. The snow sure has weighted 'em down. One good thing about it, we won't have to cut any trees when it thaws, we can just pick up all the wood we want."

"Another good thing, Pa, Sam'l won't be leaving us for a while."

"'Fraid I'm going to have to go. One man walking careful ain't as bad as two chopping and stirring up things in the woods. I'll be gone before sun-up," Sam'l said. "I've never been snowed in as comfortable before, and I will miss being with all of you. It's time, though, for me to be moving on. Don't want to wear out my welcome."

It was clear that Sam'l had made up his mind. No one argued with him. When a man had to leave, he would go, no matter what.

No one noticed Sarah's reaction. Her cheeks got pink and she felt a funny sensation. She wondered what was happening to her.

Little Deer climbed to the loft and made his plans. He, too, had decided. Surely, a boy would disturb the branches even less than a man. He would follow Sam'l's tracks. That way he would not leave a trail to follow. He went to his treasures' hiding place. Everything was ready. He would leave as soon as he could follow Sam'l.

Again that night, the men talked after supper. Little Deer looked through the crack in the loft floor. He wanted to firmly fix in his memory the picture of this place as his place. The fireplace, table, chairs, and all the furs. These people were also his people. He would miss them—but he must leave.

Little Deer hardly slept. He wanted to be sure that he was awake when Sam'l left. Long before daybreak he heard faint sounds coming from the cabin below him. There was a quiet murmur of men's voices and the soft sound of the cabin door opening and closing. A rush of cold air told him that Sam'l had gone. Luke was up and had gone outside with him. This was the only chance Little Deer would have to get out of the loft without Luke knowing it. He picked up his bundle and swiftly went down the ladder. He went over to the big iron kettle that stood in the corner next to the fireplace and put a package into it. Almost soundlessly, he crept to the door. Carefully, he eased it open just far enough to get out. He darted over to the woodpile and crouched behind it, waiting for Luke to come back to the cabin. It seemed ages until Luke returned and went inside.

Little Deer waited until he thought Luke had gone back to sleep, then he came out from behind the logs and headed in the direction that Sam'l had taken. For once, Digger didn't bark at him. He was soon in the woods, trotting down the trail that was leading him away from his dread of Boston—and away from the home and family he had grown to love.

CHAPTER EIGHTEEN

DANGEROUS TRAIL

"Little Deer sure is sleeping late. Wonder if he's sick from being down at the creek in the cold and wet yesterday?" Sarah worried as she looked up form the cornmeal mush she was frying in the skillet.

"Looked like he was all bunched up under his blanket when I came down," Nathan answered.

"Well, this mush is ready. I want to get the stew started soon's we finish eating and cleaning up. He'll have to get up now."

"He'll smell the mush and be down in a minute," Luke said as he helped himself to the food. "Sure is good, Sarah. I'm going to get all I want right now. Little Deer loves mush better than anything else you cook. I believe he'd eat it every meal if you'd make it."

"I made it special because he likes it so. I was so out of sorts at him yesterday, I thought I'd do something nice to make up for it."

They finished eating, and Little Deer still had not come down. "Nathan, you go up and see if he's sick," Sarah said as she began to clear the table.

197

Nathan climbed up to the loft and pulled back the blanket.

"Pa! Pa! He ain't here! There's just a bundle of skins pushed up under his blanket."

Luke was dumbfounded. He hurried up the ladder to look.

"Pa! Come down here. Look what's in the stew kettle!" Sarah called from below.

Luke and Nathan came down the ladder and looked at the skin-wrapped bundle that Sarah had just opened. Inside it were four beautifully carved maple bowls.

"Just look at them, Pa. Here's one that must be yours. It's got a man on it skinning a wild boar. Look, it's even got tiny tusks. This one has to be mine. It's got me sweeping. And this here's Nathan's. He's sitting on a rock with a fishing pole in his hand.

"What's the fourth one, Sarah? It has to be Little Deer's."

"Oh, Nathan, it's so sad. It's a family. There's Pa and me and you and a little boy. We're standing on each side of the boy and Pa's in back of him.

"What's sad about that? Shows that Little Deer feels like he belongs to us."

"But he's gone, Nathan, he's gone!"

"He still feels like family."

"Nathan, he never finished the little boy. He didn't carve out his face!" Sarah began to cry. "Poor, lost little boy. It's kind of like he ain't sure of who he is," Sarah sobbed. "Pa, you've got to get him back!"

"Now, Sarah, don't take on so. Maybe he didn't have time to finish it," Luke tried to comfort her.

"He had time, Pa. Where the face should be is polished smooth as silk, just like the rest of the bowl. Bring him home, Pa. Hurry, before something happens to him."

"I'm going to, Sarah. I'll find him." Luke took his rifle and got ready to go out into the cold.

"I'll go with you, Pa." Nathan said.

"No, you stay here with Sarah. This is something I got to do alone. He can't have got too far in this snow, 'less he went with Sam'l. I know he wouldn't do that, 'cause he never did take to Sam'l."

Luke went out and studied the area around the cabin. He saw the tracks he and Sam'l had made going up to the woods. There were no fresh tracks there, nor were there any on the day-old trail to the creek that Little Deer and Nathan had made. Except for a path to the woodpile, the only other tracks were those he himself had made that morning when he walked as far as the trees with Sam'l. There, on Sam'l's tracks, were the tracks of the little boy! Little Deer had gone that way. Luke wondered what he planned to do. He knew that the child wasn't trying to catch up with Sam'l. There was only one way to find out. He'd follow the trail.

Cautiously, he started into the woods. Around him in the forest he could hear the creaking and groaning of the snow-laden branches. Far off, he heard a crack and crash as one fell. He was glad he wasn't under it. By the way the trail wound, he could see that Sam'l, too, had taken care to avoid any limbs that looked too weak to support their burden of snow. It wouldn't do to be caught under that weight.

Luke walked for more than an hour. There was just the one trail through the snow. It was hard to distinguish if Little Deer's footprints were still on Sam'l's. Perhaps he'd been wrong. Maybe Little Deer had found some place to hide and was back somewhere in the clearing. He'd looked everywhere he could think of, and he'd studied the tracks. As far as he could tell, Little Deer had taken this trail. But he knew Little Deer was very clever. He'd go on for a while longer. Surely there'd be some sign that showed him clearly that the boy had come this way.

Reason told him that Little Deer was out there somewhere, but the signs were very difficult to read. Luke continued his tracking for another hour, by which time he was about to decide that he had made some mistake and turn back. Luke stopped to knock the packed snow from his feet. As he rose up he saw a handprint in the snow. It was too small to be Sam'l's. Yes, Little Deer was on this trail. Another branch fell, behind him and off to the left. The sound of it echoed through the cold, still air and snapped Luke back into his resolve to find the youngster.

Finally, a mile or so farther down the trail, the footprint paths branched. A line of small footprints veered off to the left. Luke knew that he was right, that it was Little Deer who had made the trail—and not too long ago. Little Deer wasn't as careful as Sam'l had been in his choice of route. This was downright dangerous. Why hadn't the boy been more careful? Luke decided to keep the child's trail in sight, but he chose a more cautious route. It was hard going. "I've been easy enough on him. This time he's goin' to learn a lesson. He won't worry me again when I get through with him," he promised himself.

Suddenly he stopped. Coming through the forest was the sound of a flute. "What in tarnation is that?" It was strange. "Who'd be playing a flute in a snowy woods like this?"

His skin prickled and, throwing caution to the winds, he started at a run down Little Deer's trail. He could go no farther. A large branch blocked him. Coming from the branch was the music.

He ran around the branch and tried to raise it. The music stopped and a tearful voice cried, "Pa!"

Little Deer was trapped. "Son! Son! I'm here. I'll get you out. Are you hurt?" Luke called.

"Leg stuck, Pa."

Luke worked to free the boy. He used a branch as a lever and finally raised the heavy limb enough so that the child lay free. "Crawl out, Little Deer. I can't hold this log up all day."

"Leg hurt." Slowly, the boy inched his way out, using his elbows and dragging the leg, which lay at a peculiar angle.

Finally, he was free. Luke examined the leg. "It's broke bad. I'll have to fix a splint." He cut two straight branches from the tree that had lain across the boy. Then, with his knife, he cut strips of leather from the bottom of his buckskin shirt.

"I'm going to hurt you again. I'll have to pull your leg straight. It'll hurt like fury. Here, bite on the handle of this knife."

"No. Play flute." Little Deer began to play. This time the notes that came out were not soothing. They screeched and screamed from the flute as Luke set the leg. Once the splint was in place, the flute was quiet.

"You made that sound like a cave full of fighting wildcats," Luke said. "I know it hurt. You sure are a brave one." Luke reached down and patted the child's head.

Little Deer looked up at him with pain-filled eyes. "Hurt bad, Pa. What we do now?"

"Well, I guess I'll use the lesson you taught me on the boar hunt. I'll fix a carrier like we put the meat on and haul you back home. It ain't going to be easy on you. I'll jostle you a lot. Think you can stand it?"

"Yes, Pa." Little Deer could stand anything. This was the second time Luke had saved his life. Now he doubly owed him. It was a bond that he'd never break. He'd find some way to stay with Pa. He didn't know how yet, but he would find a way.

CHAPTER NINETEEN

RECOVERY

"**H**e's getting better now, Pa," Sarah said. She looked up from the bed, where she'd been feeding soup to Little Deer. "He sure was sick from being in the weather so long like he was. Now his fever's broke and he's eating."

Luke came over to the bed and felt of the child's head. It felt cool and moist to the touch. Luke breathed a sigh of relief.

"He's had himself a time. He never let out a sound all the way back to the cabin, just kept playing that flute. Guess it took his mind off the pain and the cold."

Little Deer's eyes closed and he went to sleep.

"That's good. He'll rest now and start getting his strength back. Don't he look like an angel, Pa, laying there with that yellow hair curlin' 'round his face? I'm so glad he's home." Sarah gently brushed the hair back from the child's forehead and pulled Gramma's quilt up to the boy's chin, tucking him in snugly against the cold.

"Sarah, you're hovering over him like a hen with one chick. Let the child sleep. He ain't going nowhere the way his leg is trussed up. You've sure changed. One day you're ready to skin him alive, and the next you're treating him like one of the family."

"He is one of the family. I'm going to make up for the way I treated him before he ran off. I thought he was being mean. 'Stead, he was trying to show me every way he could that he was wantin' to be friends. Oh, Pa, how could I have been so blind? I guess it was the bowl that had him without a face on it that showed me how hard he was trying."

"I don't know which is worse, Sarah, not to know for sure *who* you are or *what* you are."

"Sometimes, Pa, who you are gets bogged down in what you let yourself be. Guess I set too much store by wanting things nice, like Ma would have fixed 'em for you. I ain't Ma. I can never take her place. Guess I tried too hard."

"You're doing fine, daughter. You ain't swept the floor once today."

"I'll always like things to be clean and nice, but I'm trying to learn not to make other people miserable making 'em that way. It ain't goin' to be easy to change, but I'm working on it."

"I know you are, Sarah, and I appreciate what you do."

"Well, nobody's tracked anything in today," Sarah stated, matter-of-factly. Then she laughed to herself. "Guess it'll take some time, Pa. Be patient with me. I've got a lot of learnin' to do."

"You got a lot of living to do yet, too," Luke said.

Sarah wondered what he meant by that. Then she asked, "Pa, can I ask you some questions?"

"Sure, Sarah, what's on your mind?"

"Pa, how old is Sam'l?"

"I don't rightly know, he's younger than me, but I don't know how much."

"Do you know if he has been married?"

"I don't know that either. Why the interest in Sam'l?"

"Oh, I don't know, Pa. Sam'l's a nice man."

Both were quiet for a while, then Sarah said, "We'd better get some sleep, Pa. I'm tired, and I know you are, too. It's been a long, hard time." Sarah got Little Deer's blanket and rolled up in it before the fire. She was soon fast asleep.

Luke sat on the bench and looked at the flames leaping from the log. He pondered the short conversation he just had with Sarah. He knew his little daughter was growing up. He shook his head, then he decided that he would build that other bed Sarah had been wanting. Since she had insisted upon putting Little Deer in her bed, she had been sleeping on the floor. She had nursed the boy through his fever, and she had not slept except for an hour or two at a time. Luke knew that it had been for love of the child, though Sarah thought she'd only been doing her duty by him. The turning point was when Little Deer was out of his head with the fever and had cried out for her. She had cradled him in her arms and rocked him back and forth, singing to him until he quieted.

Little Deer stirred upon his bed. Instantly, Luke was on his feet and went to him.

"Water," he said. Luke brought the dipper to him and helped him drink.

"Thank you, Pa." Little Deer lay back, almost instantly asleep again. The words echoed in Luke's head. Especially the "Pa." How could he send the child to the alien world of Boston? He loved him like a son. Would he send Nathan off like that? No! He made up his mind to try by every means possible to keep the boy here where he belonged.

Satisfied with his decision, Luke, too, went to sleep.

In the morning, Luke looked out at the dripping world. The snow was melting. Soon it would be spring and the gap would be open to travelers. He must come up with a plan. While he thought, he started squaring the corner pole for another bed. Not only did Sarah need it, but the guests they were expecting would need a place to sleep. He certainly wasn't anxious for them to come. Like Little Deer, Luke also wished he had never heard of Boston.

CHAPTER TWENTY

LUCAS

"Looks like spring's coming. I saw some dandelions comin' up. They're just peeping out of the ground," Luke announced as he came into the cabin. "It's about time we try out that leg, Little Deer. It should be mended by now. Let's get that splint off and see how your leg holds up."

"Pa not call me Little Deer. Me, Lucas," the child answered.

"What? Is that your name?" questioned Luke.

"Yes, me Lucas," firmly answered the boy.

"If that's what you want to be called, then Lucas it is. You'll have to remind us to call you Lucas. We're used to Little Deer.

"Little Deer gone. Now Lucas," affirmed the child.

"All right, Lucas, Let's get the splint off and see if you can stand up. It's time enough that the bone is mended."

"Me . . . I," he corrected himself, "I stand." He was working hard at speaking like they did.

"At the rate you're going, you'll be a credit to your uncle when he gets here. You're beginning to talk better than I do." Luke said.

The splint was off, and the child put both feet on the floor. He had expected to walk as he usually did and was surprised that his leg would not support his weight. He fell to the floor. Sarah went to help him up.

"No, I get up. I walk," he said firmly. He struggled to get to his feet. Sarah held herself back. He was so small and tried so hard.

"Little Deer . . . Lucas," she said, "If you hold onto the bed, you can pull yourself up." It was all she could do to keep herself from going to him, but she knew that would hurt his pride. She was learning, also. It was a hard lesson.

Finally, he struggled to his feet. He took one step on the weak leg and fell again. This time, Luke stepped in. "Tomorrow you can try again. You can't expect to do it the first time," he said as he scooped up the child in his arms, gave him a hug, and put him on the bed. "You'll be walking good before your uncle gets here. Maybe I can make you a crutch to use until you get some strength in that leg."

It was hard to remember to call Little Deer "Lucas." Since his fever, he had insisted that he was Lucas, not Little Deer. Sarah wondered if that might really be his name, or if he just worshipped Pa so much that he had used his name. But how in the world did he ever come up with Lucas, she wondered. Pa's name was Luke.

To pass the time and to amuse himself, the child played the flute. Sarah had sung to him all the songs she could remember, and he could play the melodies back to her.

"I'm goin' to have to make you a new flute. You've worn out yours and mine, too." Nathan said one day.

"Make me one, too," Sarah said. "Lucas is going to teach me to play it."

"Sarah, you don't have time for flute playing."

"I'm going to take time," she stated firmly.

"Oh, all right. Soon's the reeds are right, I'll make you a flute, too."

"Think I'll try my hand at making an autoharp like your Ma used to play," said Luke. "I believe that Lucas could learn to play that, too, seeing as how he can play that flute so good. I'm hankering to hear an autoharp again before I die."

Alarmed, Lucas cried, "You no die, Pa!"

Sarah, too, gasped a small amount of air at the thought of her father dying.

"No, No, Lucas, not for a long while, I hope. You're doing good on that leg. Ain't even limping like you used to. Won't be long and you'll be hopping around here like a rabbit again."

That puzzled the boy. How could he hop like a rabbit? A rabbit has four legs. He had only two. It must be one of Pa's jokes, he decided. But it gave him an idea. He could hop on his one good leg. He was tired of being in bed all the time. After a while, he'd try. It would be good to be able to get around by himself. When the splint was on his leg, he'd had to be carried. Now it was time for him to move about on his own legs. Maybe he could even hop to the honey pot.

He grinned at the thought of licking the golden honey from his fingers and letting it melt in his mouth. Sarah thought that Nathan was the one getting into it. She blamed him because he loved sweets so much. She never had caught him, though, and Nathan wouldn't tell on his brother. It was still a mystery to her.

Let her wonder, thought Lucas. It will give her something to think about besides cleaning and cooking. He grinned again. As soon as he could, he'd get himself some honey.

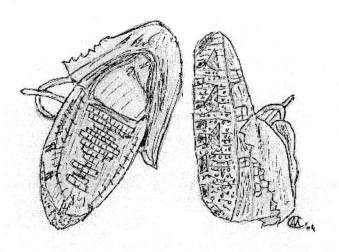

CHAPTER TWENTY-ONE

A BROTHER FOR DIGGER

"Pa, Sam'l coming and he's dragging something again. Wonder what he's got on the end of his rope this time?"

Sarah left the spring greens she was cleaning and went to meet the visitor.

"What you got there, Sam'l?" she called.

"The orneriest critter I've ever seen. It won't walk and it won't be carried. Walking, it stops to eat everything in sight. Carried, it kicks and cries. It's worse than bringing in Little Deer."

"His name is Lucas now, Sam'l."

"Lucas! Who came up with that name?"

Quickly, Sarah explained about the accident and the fever that the child had after it. "Guess it was lung fever. We almost lost him," she finished.

"You may be losing him soon. The gap is open through the mountains. A trapper came in the other day and said it was passable now. Guess Little Deer's uncle will be coming before long."

"Lucas," Sarah corrected him.

"All right . . . Lucas. It ain't easy to get used to."

It seemed to Sarah that the day had darkened. She didn't want that uncle to come. She didn't even want to think about him.

Sam'l tugged at the rope. "Here, do something with this animal 'fore I lose my patience completely." From behind the bush came a feeble, "Baaa!"

"Why, it's a lamb? Where did you get it, Sam'l?"

"Family stopped at the fort last fall with some sheep they was driving. A ewe dropped this lamb just before they was fixing to go on after the snow melted. It was a runt and wouldn't hold up on the trail. I took it off their hands. It wasn't big enough to eat, so I thought I'd try my hand at raising it. Did such a good job, it thinks I'm its mother." He pushed away the soft nose that poked at him. "I ain't got time to fool with it now. Thought you'd tend to it for me."

"Oh, Sam'l! I'll tend to it so good you won't know it when you get back." Sarah hugged the lamb. His wool would make them stockings and mittens and caps. She was so excited that she forgot about the gap in the mountains being open.

"Nathan, Lucas, Pa, look! See what Sam'l's brought!" she called to them as they came from the field.

After greeting Sam'l and admiring his gift, Luke said, "That critter's goin' to need a pen. He'll eat everything in your garden if he ain't fenced, Sarah. It ain't right to keep him tied on the end of a rope. You boys see if you can figure out a way to pen him. Give him some shade and plenty of room to run."

Lucas and Nathan went to do as Luke had said. Sam'l tied the lamb to a tree, and Sarah went back to her greens. Luke and Sam'l sat under another tree to talk.

"I ain't looking forward to your next visit, Sam'l, when you bring that uncle to take the boy away. Lucas is just like one of us now. Even Sarah feels that way. I hate to see him going off to a big city he won't like. Seems like the boy's been through enough in his short life, without having this added, too."

"I don't know what you can do about it, Luke. The boy's blood kin have a right to him. You're not related to him by nothing."

"Nothing but love, Sam'l. That should count for something."

"Short of running off with him somewhere, I don't know what you can do to keep him."

"I hate to lose him so much that I even thought about doing that."

"How does the boy feel?" Sam'l asked.

"He says he ain't going. He's run off to keep from goin'. That's how he broke his leg."

"I know. Sarah told me about it."

"I been studying on it more than I like to admit. I just ain't come up with nothing."

"There ain't nothing, Luke. You might as well face it. He's got to go back."

"I know, Sam'l. That don't mean I got to like it."

"Let's go to the field, Luke. We ain't doing no good talking about it. We can help the boys get that pen going and the fence put up. Look's like they've already got a good bunch of saplings cut for rails."

"Where you headed from here, Sam'l?"

"Going north for a while. Thought I'd scout out the Indians a bit. See if they're still as peaceful as they seem to be. I like to know for myself. Let's get to work. I'll be setting out in the morning, but I'll help you all I can today."

"Can you talk to the Shawnee?"

"I know some Shawnee words, and I know their sign language. I feel safe in Indian country."

Luke shook his head, not understanding Sam'l's desire to explore Indian country. He changed the subject. "Sarah sure was happy with the lamb. Guess she'll be pestering me next to build her a loom. Next winter, she can keep her mind off losing Lucas by weaving and knitting. She'll have flax and wool to work up."

"Luke, Sarah works hard beyond her years. She'll be wanting a spinning wheel, too. You wait on that a while, Luke. I been working on one for her."

"Sam'l, you're just spoiling her. Every time you come, she'll expect you to be bringing something."

"Well, I had to do something during the winter to keep busy. Since I ain't got no woman fussing at me or cleaning under my feet, I had time on my hands. There was some pretty wild cherry wood I had seasoning. Wasn't no need for it to go to waste. I'll bring the spinning wheel next time I come."

"That'll sure help her when the boy has to go, Sam'l. You're just like family to us."

"You and your young'uns are all the family I got. It pleasures me to do something for them."

"You sure please Sarah. I can tell by how she looks at you. And look at her over there, mothering that lamb. She's hand-feeding it greens. Bet she washed 'em first." Luke laughed.

Sarah had one arm around the lamb. In her other hand she held fresh leaves for it to nibble. "You're just the softest, sweetest little lamb I've ever seen," she whispered to it.

The lamb nibbled diligently on the greens. "Come here, Digger," she called to the dog. "Meet your new brother. Seems like all we get around here is boy types. It'd be nice not to be the only girl around here for a change."

The dog sniffed cautiously at the wooly stranger. He wasn't sure what to make of it. He lay at Sarah's feet and watched to see what it would do. He didn't give his friendship carelessly.

"You're going to have to have a name. Maybe Nathan will come up with one for you, like he did for Digger," Sarah told the lamb. "I'll see to it that you get plenty to eat."

Overhearing his daughter's conversation with the animal, Luke, raising his voice a bit, called over to her, "He'll probably be the only lamb in these parts, and we're as hungry as he is. What's there to eat, Sarah? I do believe that lamb has made you forget all about the rest of us."

"Oh, Pa, supper's cooking. I ain't likely to forget to feed you. Let's go inside. You all get your hands washed and we can eat."

"It's plain the lamb didn't make you forget about washing hands," remarked Sam'l, smiling at Sarah.

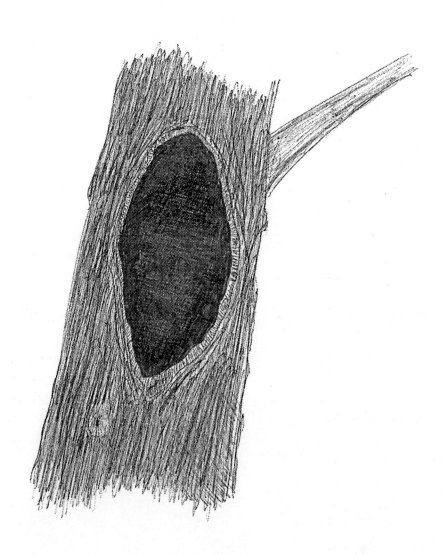

CHAPTER TWENTY-TWO

AT THE HONEY TREE

"Boys, I spotted a swarm of bees back up on the far side of the slope. They looked to be headed for that old poplar tree that was hit by lightning. It seems a likely place for them to make honey. You've worked hard and have earned a treat. Tomorrow you can go up there and rob the bees. Just be sure you leave then enough honey to live on until they can make more," Luke cautioned them.

Nathan and Lucas looked at each other and grinned. A whole day of honey! They went up to the loft to make their plans and gather what they needed. Lucas tucked his reed flute into the front of his shirt. Unless he was working in the fields, he rarely left the cabin without it. Next to Nathan, it was his best friend.

The next morning, they left the cabin early. Sarah had prepared a packet of food for them but, in their haste, they had left it on the trestle table. When they stopped at a stream for a cool drink of water, they remembered it.

"Sarah will be upset that we forgot the food," commented Nathan, "but she'll know that we won't go hungry. We can make a spear and get a squirrel or rabbit like you did for her when you first came, Little . . . ahh . . . Lucas." It was hard to remember not to call him Little Deer.

"We'll never go hungry, Nathan. There's food everywhere."

Lucas had worked hard on speaking as he heard Pa, Nathan and Sarah speak. Sometimes he had to search for a word he wanted to use, but those times were becoming fewer and fewer.

When they reached the tree Pa had told them about, they began to gather twigs and leaves to build a smudge fire to smoke out the bees. Neither of the boys wished to anger them; the resulting bee stings would be painful, indeed, although both boys agreed that the honey was worth it.

While the smoke was rising, they sat at the foot of the tree and whittled on small spears they could use to catch a small animal.

"Lucas, I sure am going to miss you when your uncle comes to take you to Boston," Nathan said.

"I ain't goin', Nathan. I'll run and hide where nobody can find me. You are my family. This is my home. I ain't going!"

"But your real family wants you to come and live with them. You'll live in a big, fancy house, and have cake to eat every day, and maybe ride in a buggy, and sleep in a big, soft feather bed, and go to a real school."

Everything that Nathan described made Lucas more determined not to go to Boston. "Nathan, I don't know what a city is. I don't know what cake is. Is it like Sarah's cornbread?"

"Better. But don't you want to be with your real family?"

"You, Sarah, and Pa are my real family. I owe Pa my life. I can't leave. I'm not going."

Lucas stood up. "Let's go and get a squirrel. We can cook it while the bees are getting smoked out."

After a successful hunt, they sat at a small fire and finished eating the last of the squirrel. Lucas licked his fingers, wiped them on his smoky shirt, and pulled his flute from it. He leaned back against the tree and began to play. First, the sounds he made were like the rustle of wind through the trees, then he played sounds of the forest. His music changed from a soothing melody to the cries of animals in pain. He stopped suddenly on a note that sounded like a cry of death.

"Let's go home," he said, standing up. "Pa will be wondering where we are."

CHAPTER TWENTY-THREE

ARRIVALS FROM THE EAST

"Sam'l, there's someone looking for you," James called as Sam'l walked into the settlement.

Sam'l went over to where James stood with two men who were strangers to the territory. The younger man was dressed in buckskins and wore them as though he felt good in them. The older, smaller man was dressed in a dusty, black wool suit at which he continually brushed with his hat. He twitched his nose in distaste as Sam'l approached.

Sam'l slung the pack of partly cleaned squirrels and rabbits from his shoulders. He handed them to James and said, "Here, give these to Martha. I reckon she can find a use for them. I'd have cleaned them better, but I got word about an Indian attack, so I came as fast as I could. It don't appear I needed to be in such a hurry."

"I'm sorry the message wasn't more clear, Sam'l. I'm afraid you fretted without need to. I should have come for you myself, but I've been trying to explain to Mr. Peabody why Little Deer isn't here at the settlement. He seems to think we should send for the child to come to the fort, since Mr. Peabody has already come all the way from Boston. He's a little put out that we're causing him all this trouble."

"He looks like he is in some hurry, too," observed Sam'l. "He seems quite impatient."

"He is, Sam'l. He must be pretty important back in Boston. He tells that he quit teaching and went into banking. He wants to get back to Boston to his business."

James and Sam'l walked over to the two men. "Sam'l, this is Mr. Henry Peabody. He's the brother of Little Deer's father," said James.

"If you refer to my brother's child, please do so in a Christian manner. His name is Abner. Abner Horatio Peabody III, heir to the family fortune and bearer of the proudest name in Boston."

Sam'l looked at James, but James was looking at the sky.

"Mr. Sam'l, if you please, go and return as soon as possible with the child. From the evidence, sketchy though it has been in spite of my repeated requests for verification, this child appears to be the boy I am seeking."

Sam'l face reddened. "I don't believe I'll do that, but I will take you to the place where the lad is staying."

Undaunted, Mr. Peabody continued, "It does seem that even in the wilderness there should be at least one person who could correspond in an intelligent manner. That child should be here to greet me."

"Oh, for heaven's sake, Henry. These men aren't impressed with you," said the buckskin clad man at Peabody's side. Then he turned to Sam'l, extended his hand and said, "I'm Adam Blake. Thank God, I'm only a half-brother to Henry, and I wish it were even less."

Sam'l shook Adam's hand and said, "I'm proud to make your acquaintance."

Adam continued, "Actually, he's not as bad as he sounds. He's just used to people bowing and scraping in front of him, and he's not sure how to act when it doesn't happen. What do you suggest we do to get the boy?"

Sam'l liked Adam immediately. He smiled and said, "First, we get your brother into some clothes that won't tear from going through the woods. Then we need to stop at my place for me to pick up some things I need to take to Sarah. Then we will walk out to Luke's place."

"Is it a difficult trip . . . I mean, for Henry?"

"It ain't going to be pleasant getting there—or after we get there." Sam'l ignored Henry and spoke directly to Adam.

Sam'l's shoulders were set in a way that showed his contempt for Henry as he spoke to Adam. Adam could see by Sam'l's set jaw that he would have to step in between Henry and Sam'l often. Sam'l would delay the inevitable as long as possible by going to his cabin first, then to Luke's. It would make the trip twice as long and twice as uncomfortable.

After some buckskins were borrowed for Henry and altered to his critical satisfaction by Martha, they set out for Sam'l's cabin. As usual, Martha sent a small package for Sarah.

"These buckskins itch and they smell horrible," Henry complained.

"These buckskins are cumbersome and hard to walk in," Henry complained again.

Sam'l gritted his teeth. He imagined stripping the buckskins off Henry's bony body and running him naked through the woods. He grinned at the prospect of doing that. Instead, Sam'l led them through the roughest, thorniest trail he could find. Adam cheerfully followed him, quickly learning to identify trees and edible roots and berries as they traveled. He marveled at the number of small animals they saw and gloried in the songs of the birds. Soon he was imitating many of them and laughed when a confused bird answered his call.

Late in the day, after Sam'l had set up a campsite for them, Adam said, "Sam'l, this is heaven!"

"I always knowed it, Adam." Sam'l answered.

As they sat down to their dinner, Adam asked, "Show me again how to tie that loop you use to snare the rabbit. I want to learn everything I can."

Sam'l was pleased that Adam was showing an interest in his country. An immediate kinship grew between them.

"Adam,' barked Henry, "there is no need for you to allow your enthusiasm for such a savage existence to overtake your good manners."

"Henry, I can see why people are moving to Kentucky. This place is a paradise."

After they had eaten, Henry's patience was wearing thin, and he said, "Rubbish, Adam. Perhaps you and Mr. Sam'l would like to rest. I would appreciate the quiet while I read my nightly passages from the Bible."

"Adam, we better get some sleep. It's a long way yet, but we will get to Luke's tomorrow. I've enjoyed your company. You'd make a good woodsman," Sam'l said, ignoring Henry.

"And I've enjoyed your company, too, Sam'l."

CHAPTER TWENTY FOUR

MR. HENRY PEABODY

The corn was growing tall. Sarah had planted her gourds next to the stoop, and the flowers looked like yellow stars against the rustic, gray logs of the cabin. The young flax in the field waved in the soft, summer breeze. Bees flitted from flower to flower and hurried back to their hiding places with the nectar.

Sarah was restless. She was constantly watching the woods, dreading Sam'l's return. When he came, she knew that Lucas would have to leave them and go with his uncle. How she would miss the boy! He was like her little brother. She could hardly bear the thought of him not being with them. "Drat!" she said, wiping a tear from her eye.

Nibbles, the lamb, played inside his fence. He was growing. Next spring, when they sheared him, he would give much wool. Also, thankfully, he and Digger got along well together.

Everything was so pleasant, so idyllic. Why did things have to change? "Drat!" she grumbled again.

Sarah went into the cabin and brought out the blankets to air. Every time she hung them over the bushes, she thought about finding Gramma's quilt. There were still places to fix where the fabric had rotted in the weather. With the linen she could weave from the flax—and the wool from Nibbles—she could soon fill in the missing pieces. She would wait, though, until the pieces told more of her life history. She stood touching Gramma's quilt. "Gramma," she said out loud,   "I've only got the piece of dress from Martha. The only history I've got was part of the clothing I wore in the Indian village, and I really don't want to remember that."

"Sarah," Luke came up to her. "They're here. It's time." There were tears in his eyes. "Sam'l's coming through the woods. He's got two men with him."

"Oh, Pa! No! Not so soon! I ain't ready for them." She started to cry.

"Well, ready or not, they're here. Don't make it any harder on Lucas than it already is. I've got to go out to meet 'em. I'd rather be strung up by my thumbs than go out there."

"Does Nathan know they're coming?"

"No. He and Lucas are in the woods robbing the bee tree of honey. They won't be back for a while. They got to smoke out the bees before they can get the honey. Better have some mud ready. They'll be stung plenty before it's over."

"Lucas will do anything for honey. I saw him at the honey bucket, but I didn't let on I knew. I'm afraid it'll be a long time before he gets any more." Sarah continued crying softly.

"Come now, Sarah. That ain't no way to greet strangers. I'll go meet them. Wash your face, and come out when you're ready. Sam'l's bringing you something that'll make you feel better."

"Ain't nothing could make me feel good about losing Lucas," she sobbed.

"Straighten up, Sarah," Luke said, harshly. "You knew it was coming. It's here. We'll have to face it." Luke, masking his own sorrow, patted her shoulder and went out to meet Sam'l.

"I brought Sarah's spinning wheel, Luke," Sam'l greeted him.

"That's wonderful, Sam'l. I hope it helps. She ain't really happy at the moment."

Luke turned to the men with Sam'l. He knew immediately that the short man with glasses wearing the buckskins as though they offended him was Mr. Henry Peabody. His companion was tall, muscular, and seemed to fit in with the surrounding wilderness.

"This here's Mr. Henry Peabody and his brother Adam, Luke."

"Half brother," Adam interjected.

Luke spoke, "I can't honestly say that I'm pleased to see you here. We sure don't want Lucas to go."

"Lucas? Oh, I assume that you refer to Abner, the son of my deceased brother, whom we have come to take back to Boston where he belongs."

Digger shared Luke's feelings. The hackles on the dog's neck rose and he growled as Mr. Peabody passed him.

"I hope that beast is tamed!" Henry said as he glanced at Digger. "I trust that the boy is well and able to travel. We will leave for civilization as soon as possible. This wilderness isn't fit for any man."

"Henry, I don't see why you're in such a hurry to leave this paradise. I ain't," Adam spoke up.

"Am not, not 'ain't', Adam," corrected the little man, stiffly. "You seem to be using the dialect of the area lately." He glanced at Sam'l.

"Samuel, if you will be good enough to show us to our quarters, I should like to rest before dinner."

"Oh, Henry, get off your high horse. You've been in the wilderness before. You know how it is. Why don't your just admit that you aren't looking forward to this meeting with your nephew, who you don't really know and who you don't really want?" Adam confronted Henry.

"Then leave him here. We do want him!" Luke blurted.

"Preposterous! He is a Peabody, and he shall be reared to carry on the name. I owe that to my brother, God rest his soul."

Luke could see that this situation would be worse than he had expected. This man would make Lucas miserable.

Sam'l just shrugged his shoulders as he looked at Luke. There was nothing he could do.

"Well, come to the cabin. We'll make you as comfortable as we can. Sarah will be around shortly," Luke said crisply.

"Where is my nephew? He should be here to greet me."

"He and Nathan are out robbing the bees of their honey. They'll be back when they get here."

"Aren't you concerned about the Indians? This is a child of nine years."

"He's well able to care for himself. Remember, he lived with the Indians for most of his life." The more Luke heard, the less he liked Henry Peabody. "Here's Sarah."

"I brought you a present, Sarah." Sam'l said as he pointed to the spinning wheel.

"It's lovely, Sam'l. I'll thank you properly later," she answered in a dead voice.

"Sarah, this is Mr. Peabody and his brother Adam."

So this skinny, dried-up little man was Lucas's uncle. She looked at him and then remembered her manners. "How do you do?" she dropped a swift curtsy.

Taken aback at her manners, Mr. Peabody said, "Pleased to meet you, Miss --?"

"Just Sarah. I ain't old enough to be Miss anything yet."

"Hello, Sarah, I'm Adam," he stepped forward, shook her hand, and held it for an unusually long time. "You have the neatest, cleanest cabin I've ever seen. The gourds at the door look very pretty."

Sarah's mouth fell open. Adam was the handsomest man that Sarah had seen in a very long while. She wanted to say something, but no words would come out.

Adam continued, "You'll have to make allowances for Henry. He's scared but won't admit it. He don't know what to do with a child like Abner."

Sarah felt immobilized. The words wouldn't come out.

"Henry is an important man in Boston, so he can't ever be wrong. He'll do his duty to the family or die in the attempt."

Sarah didn't want to think of Lucas's leaving. She changed the subject. "Well, supper's ready. I'm sure you are hungry from your long walk from the fort."

"Should we wait for the boys?" Adam asked.

"It's ready now; we should eat."

"I would prefer to wait for Abner. I am sure he would enjoy a hot meal," Henry sniveled.

Sarah bristled. "Mr. Peabody, they ain't never gone hungry, nor have they had cold food in this house. I tend them as best I can, but when supper's ready, it's ready. Let's eat."

"I appreciate your efforts, Miss Sarah," Henry said and sat down.

Sarah just pushed the food around in her bowl. She wondered how the scrawny little man could eat as much as he did. Three times she had filled his bowl, and he'd eaten all the cornbread. She'd have to make more for the boys.

"Delicious, Miss Sarah," he finally said as he pushed his bowl back. "I had forgotten how good primitive food can taste."

"Just Sarah, not Miss Sarah," she reminded him, absently. It was turning dark, and she wondered where Lucas and Nathan were. She secretly hoped they both ran off for a few days.

Finally, the door burst open and the boys came in. They were so excited they didn't notice the men as they joyously waved the honey bucket. "Full to the brim, Sarah," Nathan announced from a smoke-blackened face. "We're starving! What's for supper?"

"I want some cornbread and honey," Lucas said.

"Who are these boys?" Mr. Peabody asked.

"This is Nathan, and this one is Lucas—or Abner, as you call him," Luke said.

"That boy is not Abner!" Mr. Peabody said.

"What do you mean?" Luke asked.

Both Nathan and Lucas sat wide-eyed.

"I told you in the letter that Abner had blond hair, blue eyes, a strawberry birthmark and a twisted foot."

"So you did."

"His right foot was severely twisted at birth. When he was old enough, my brother planned to take him to Boston to see if the foot could be corrected. Don't you see, this boy's feet are both straight," Henry said angrily.

"Yes, I see that," Luke said.

"If you had read my letter carefully, you could have saved me this hazardous, foolish journey. We have wasted our time, Adam, on a wild goose chase. We have been misled. I do not know why these people used us to rid themselves of a troublesome child and get some of the family money. We will return to Boston as soon as possible."

"Yes, go," Sarah thought, nearly blurting it out aloud.

"Henry, are you sure? Abner was just a baby the last time you saw him. Children change a great deal," Adam questioned.

"Adam, did you not listen to me? Abner had a twisted foot. This imposter's feet are straight. Abner couldn't walk without limping. There is no limp when this fraud walks across the room. We are being hoodwinked. They obviously recognized the Peabody name and know of the family's financial situation. We will leave here as soon as possible," Henry sputtered.

The cabin was deathly quiet. Sarah kept her eyes on her hands in her lap. Nathan went to the stew pot and began slowly to ladle stew into his bowl. Luke and Sam'l looked everywhere but at each other. All of them ignored the insults that Henry had hurled at them. Lucas crossed his arms and pulled his shirt as tightly as he could. Even though he knew that his strawberry birthmark could not be seen, he felt as though it was glowing through the shirt.

Henry, red-faced and almost hopping with anger, choked and began to cough. Nobody pounded him on the back to help him get air. Nobody cared. Finally, the spasm stopped and he breathed in a great lungful of air. When he could speak again he said, "We leave tomorrow, Adam. If we could leave tonight, we would go now."

"You can go, Henry, but the more I see of this country, the better I like it. I think I'll stay and look around a bit. Might even stake out a claim. Delia'd probably come out and keep house for me."

"Neither you nor your sister are civilized! Do as you please! I shall return to Boston at the earliest possible opportunity. Samuel, you will escort me back to the fort in the morning. I have wasted enough time as it is. This child is not Abner," ordered Henry.

"Pa, . . ." Sarah began to speak but stopped as Luke's eyes met hers.

"Sam'l, if it won't burden you, I'll go to the fort with you and see what's around these parts. It looks like a good place to live," Adam said.

"Glad to have you, Adam. We'll leave at sun-up. The sooner we get Mr. Peabody off for Boston, the better."

*

The next morning dawned bright and clear. The three men were preparing to leave. The boys did not come down from the loft, but they were awake. Nathan held his finger up to his mouth to indicate that Lucas should be quiet. It wasn't necessary, since Lucas was being as quiet as he could be. In no way was he going down to be confronted by Mr. Peabody.

Sarah was also awake. She was hardly breathing. She had had enough of Mr. Peabody and wanted no more. Especially, she didn't want him to ask her any questions about Abner. She listened, and as soon as she heard the men leave she got up and called softly to Nathan, "Nathan, I think they're gone."

"I hope so, and I never want to see that Henry Peabody again."

"Me, neither," said the quiet voice of Lucas.

Luke, as was his custom, walked with the men to the edge of the clearing. He said, "Mr. Peabody, I'm sorry that you made this long trip for nothing." Turning to Adam, he said, "There's a piece of land about five miles that way you might want to look at. It lays good and it has water. It would pleasure us to have you as a neighbor, Adam."

Luke shook hands with Sam'l, "It is always good to see you."

Sam'l nodded, turned, and set out at a steady pace toward the fort.

Sam'l looked at Luke. Without words with Luke, Sam'l knew he would never tell Henry Peabody that until Lucas had broken his leg, his right foot had been crooked. When the splint was removed, his foot was straight.

With a light heart, Luke turned to go back to his family. From inside the cabin came the joyful melody of a reed flute.

232

EPILOG

Luke walked back to the cabin and was surprised when all three children stepped out. "Whoa, are all of you up already?

"Yes, Pa," all three said in unison.

"It's a little early for some of you. Nathan, we usually have to drag you and Lucas out of bed. Why so early?" Luke already knew the answer.

"Are we safe now, Pa?" Sarah asked.

"I really hope so. I'm ready to put this whole mess behind me."

Lucas hadn't said anything. Finally, he asked, "Can I stay, Pa."

"Yes, Pa, he can stay, can't he?" Nathan pleaded.

Luke stood up very straight, cleared his throat and said, "As far as I am concerned, this matter is closed. Mr. Peabody didn't want Lucas. He said so—we all heard him. Lucas, you have a rightful place in this family. I want you to consider yourself as my son and Sarah and Nathan your sister and brother. We will be a family." Luke couldn't contain himself. Tears rolled down his cheeks.

Lucas, only half as tall as Luke, hugged his Pa. He never said a word. He couldn't. His throat was dry and his mouth wouldn't move.

Sarah wiped the tears from her eyes. "Pa, I know we will be happy. I so want Adam and his sister to be our neighbors. I don't know her, but I really need another woman to talk to."

"Woman! Woman talk," Nathan chided.

"I know what you mean, Sarah," Luke said. "I feel like we have been through a lot, but I feel that our family will do just all right now."

"Me too, Pa. I know we will," Sarah said.

ABOUT THE AUTHORS

Elizabeth Durbin is a retired teacher. She was born in Wisconsin and because her father was an army officer the family moved often, settling finally in Bowling Green, Kentucky, where Betty earned both bachelor's and master's degrees in education at Western Kentucky University. After teaching at the university for a year, Betty began a series of assignments at military bases, first at Fort Knox, Kentucky and then at Mannheim, Germany. Returning to the States, she taught in California and finally in Kentucky for the last 24 years of her career. Her specialties were Art and English.

A mother of six, Betty first told stories then committed them to writing so her children could read them. She lives full-time in Bowling Green but spends summers at a cabin at Barren River Lake, Kentucky, a home she built from the ground up.

&

Ernest Matuschka, a Nebraskan, grew up in a small town, which afforded him the opportunity to hunt and fish as a youth.

Shortly after graduation from college, he entered the U.S. Air Force—during the Korean war—where he served as an intelligence officer.

Following his military service, he taught school in Colorado, in California and in Paris, France, where he was a guidance counselor, later moving to Germany, where he served as Director of Guidance at the Mannheim American School. It was in Germany that he met his writing partner, Elizabeth Durbin. The Durbins and the Matuschkas had ten children between them, and they (and their families) became fast friends during the two years they were together.

The Matuschkas returned to California at the end of their German experience, and, a few years later, Ernest applied for a leave of absence to complete work on his Ph.D. in clinical psychology. When he earned that degree, he and his family returned to Nebraska, where Ernest took a teaching position at the University of Nebraska at Kearney and opened a small private practice.

Ernest has written a number of professional articles for peer review psychology journals, authored two books on genealogy, and translated a book from German to English.

He retired from teaching and from practice in 1990. With their children grown and gone, the couple has spent the last decade living half time in Nebraska and half-time in Chandler, Arizona.

&

Cole Matuschka, who produced the interior text illustrations for this book, is a freelance artist in Sellersburg, Indiana, where he lives with his parents and one brother. He intends to follow his passion for art by pursuing a degree at nearby Indiana University Southeast.

For further information or to order additional copies of this volume, please contact

OPA Publishing
Box 12354
Chandler, Arizona 85248-0023

Or visit the OPA Publishing web sites at
http://www.opapublishing.com/
or
http://www.opapresents.com/

Volume Two, containing Books Three and Four, is also available on our web site.

opa

Printed in the United States
34444LVS00005B/163-180